UNDERWATER
VIBES

Visit us at www.boldstrokesbooks.com

UNDERWATER VIBES

by

Mickey Brent

2017

UNDERWATER VIBES

ISBN 13: 978-1-63555-002-3

This Trade Paperback Original Is Published By
Bold Strokes Books, Inc.
P.O. Box 249
Valley Falls, NY 12185

First Edition: November 2017

CREDITS
EDITOR: KATIA NOYES
PRODUCTION DESIGN: STACIA SEAMAN
COVER ART BY MICKEY BRENT
COVER DESIGN BY MELODY POND

Acknowledgments

This book would not have been possible without the support of my close family, friends, students, and fellow writing partners. Throughout the years, you have encouraged me as I honed my writing skills and nearly pulled out my hair to get this story "just right." Many thanks to Katia Noyes, whose editing expertise helped me polish the final manuscript, and to Melody, who designed the book cover, and Stacia, for production design. I am especially grateful to Radclyffe, Sandy, Cindy, Carsen, and everyone at Bold Strokes Books, who worked with such incredible dedication and professionalism during the publishing process. Lastly, to my readers, thank you for choosing *Underwater Vibes*—I hope you will enjoy hanging out with my characters as much as I do.

For C. TQM pour toujours.

CHAPTER ONE

One gray Saturday morning, Hélène Dupont held her breath while clutching her seat belt. The damp wind battered her cheeks as Marc's new Ferrari tore around the streets of Brussels. She stared at her husband's pale fingers grasping the wheel.

This was not the man she had married. That gentle, studious fellow had vanished, and a self-absorbed, flashy jock had surfaced in his place.

Marc whizzed past another car. Hélène pinched her lips.

Finally, the red Ferrari screeched to a halt.

"*Merde*," exclaimed Marc. "Why can't they build parking lots in Brussels like other normal cities?"

Hélène focused her eyes on a blue bird perched on a fence while Marc wedged his car into a tight parking spot, nudging the Mercedes behind them.

How she despised these early Saturday morning outings.

Marc's fingers tightened around her arm. "*M'enfin*, you're getting heavy." He thrust their fold-up grocery cart at her. "Don't forget your little-old-lady-buggy."

Resisting the urge to kick his prized Ferrari, Hélène squinted at the tight-fitting sports outfit her husband wore to show off his athletic body. She often caught him in the bathroom, admiring his muscles in the mirror. *At home, it's bad enough. Why does he have to do this here?*

In comparison, Hélène knew she wasn't exactly a beauty queen, but her closest friends led her to believe she possessed a certain bit of charm. At least she liked to think so. Especially when she dressed for special occasions, which were scarce since Marc hated to go out—except to the market on Saturdays, and the gym in the evenings.

Through her glasses, Hélène aimed her blue eyes at her husband's chin, which was chiseled and hard, like a freshly cut slab of marble. She often calculated the angle at which it stuck out, depending on his mood. She shuddered. Speaking of things that stick out…She peeked at her stomach. *C'est énorme. All I have to do is inhale, and I put on weight.*

Hélène's eyes followed Marc's white sneakers streaming across the cobblestones. She struggled to move faster, but her grocery cart had other ideas. Its flimsy wheels kept snagging the cobblestones; the more Hélène resisted, the louder they screeched.

Hélène glimpsed a homeless man in tattered clothes on the sidewalk, with a stray dog snoozing in his lap. She could barely make out the man's features under his long hair, scraggly beard, and sun-toasted face.

Marc slowed down. The dog growled. The man looked up. A dirty hand shot out toward Marc's knee.

"Bonjour, Monsieur. Got a coin to spare? I'd be much obliged."

"Mon Dieu, get a life!" hissed Marc as he stepped over ten soiled, bare toes.

Hélène fumbled in her purse. Blushing, she dropped a few coins in the man's palm. *"Je suis désolée, Monsieur.* My husband appears to be in a bad mood."

"*Merci, Madame.*" The man's weathered lips softened as he fingered the coins.

Smiling awkwardly, Hélène ran after her husband, cart in tow.

Marc whipped around. "Do we have to feed all the beggars in town?" he snapped, spitting into the gutter.

Hélène recoiled as if he had just slapped her. Bitterness filled her mouth as Marc stormed off. What had happened to the tender young man she had fallen in love with?

They had met in high school. Both bookworms, they would seek refuge in the school library. Elbows rubbing, the young couple would huddle with their textbooks on rainy Belgian afternoons. Hélène adored Latin; Marc preferred test tubes and lab rats. He sneaked her favorite Belgian chocolates, Côte d'Or noir, into the library—just for her. He was so shy then. With such a cute grin. He sat on the steps and waited—patient as a puppy—after her piano lessons, concocting silly phrases to whisper into her ear, to make her giggle.

This morning, Hélène had little time to reflect on her sweet past. She was too busy trying to keep up with Marc, zigzagging from stand to stand. Her husband had an agenda, and Hélène's task was to follow it.

The hardest part was at the baker's. Hélène's nostrils sniffed the air like a stray dog, inhaling the just-baked aroma of fresh, crusty bread. Her mouth watered just like it used to on Sunday mornings when she was a kid. Maman would let Hélène peek at her homemade rolls, lined on the hot oven tray like puffy melted sailors in white uniforms. She would hand one to her daughter, slathered with fresh unsalted butter, "just to make sure they're not poison." And if Hélène reached for a second, Maman would remind her, "Only one today, *chérie.* These have to last us the whole week."

Hélène grasped an appetizing loaf of *pain de campagne*. But just as she opened her coin purse, Marc swiped the crusty loaf from her. He grabbed another one, just like it, and placed it in the cart instead. Hélène shrugged and paid the baker, who flashed her his usual concerned look.

At the wine stand, Hélène spotted an unusual bottle. Its label had dainty yellow swirls around blue birds and tiny red flowers. The birds seemed to be jumping over the flowers. But before Hélène could place the bottle in her cart, Marc clicked his tongue.

"That's too expensive. We're getting these," he ordered, shoving two bottles of *vin de table* into the cart.

Hélène pursed her lips. *Such a killjoy.* But she wasn't in a mood to argue. Marc always won anyway. Cringing, she handed some bills to the wine seller, a distinguished, elderly gentleman from India. She had never been to India, but if everyone there was like him, she knew she would adore the country. He always wore such crisp-looking linen outfits. And even in gloomy weather, a ray of warm light radiated from his eyes. Sometimes, when the noon sun emerged through the damp Belgian clouds, if she squinted hard enough, she thought she could detect a golden aura around him.

"Anything else, *Madame?*" the elderly man asked with his peculiar, gentle accent.

Marc replied curtly, "*Non.* We're in a hurry," and turned his back on the man. Hélène smiled apologetically.

Now that Hélène's cart was loaded with groceries, it was even harder to maneuver through the marketplace. When she paused to catch her breath, her eyes smarted.

Marc raced ahead, oblivious of the sweat trickling down his wife's face.

Then he spun around. "*Non*, Hélène. *Pas encore!* You do this to me every week!"

Hélène ignored her husband's pleas and raced, cart in tow, to her favorite spot: the flower stand. She plunged into the rows of plants, popping her nose into the flowers' tender bellies, taking in their sweet nectar.

Flowers had always brought joy into Hélène's life. As she nestled her cheeks in their silkiness, her mind drifted back to summer nap times.

When Hélène was barely old enough to crawl, Maman would approach her crib and, to wake her sleeping daughter, tickle her stubby nose with flower tips. Even though little Hélène's mind was still fuzzy from her afternoon snooze, her senses fully captured the enchanting experience. The sticky scents and cheery colors sparked such curiosity in the petite *mademoiselle* that by the time she was four, she was begging Maman to introduce to her each species in their local flower shop.

Hélène's mother, a young housewife with a tight budget, did her best to honor her daughter's wishes. They checked out botany books from the library; Hélène sat in Maman's lap while the two pored over the pages, unraveling the secrets of nature.

Even now, when Hélène shut her eyes, she heard Maman's soft voice as she recited scientific explanations for each species. Her youthful, tender ears had soaked up each Latin name with its botanical description. And at age four, when Hélène grew nearsighted, she would press her face to the books to memorize their glossy pictures. She could still remember the odor of the slightly mildewed pages.

Now, as Hélène drifted amongst hundreds of plant species, once more, she immersed herself in the mysterious world of floral sensations.

Marc rapped his knuckles on a wooden sign displaying various plant prices. "What a rip-off!" After no response from his wife, he rapped again. "You're such a pain, Hélène. *Je te jure.*"

Hélène lifted her face from a tuft of orange blossoms. Gesturing toward the opposite end of the market, she proposed, "*D'accord*, Marc. Why don't you go order your beer, and I'll meet you—"

"Don't take all day!" interrupted Marc, dashing off with the grocery cart. When it hit a jagged cobblestone, a ripe tomato bounced out. "*Merde!*" he snarled as it rolled away.

"Be there in a minute!" muttered Hélène, ignoring her husband's remarks as he stormed toward their usual café. The delicious orange flowers had captured all her attention.

❖

Sylvie Routard, a young, dark-haired woman, happened to be standing a few feet away from the couple, behind the shadows of a massive tree. When the man raised his voice, she peeked to see who was hurling such offensive snarls, and at whom. When she saw the man hit the sign with his knuckles, she winced. *What a brute.*

Then her eyes fell on the blond woman in a loose skirt and glasses. The expression on her face resembled a lost bird. *She doesn't deserve this kind of treatment. Nobody does. Who does this jerk think he is, anyway?*

Pressing her face against the rough tree trunk, Sylvie cocked her ear to catch the couple's conversation. When she saw the man abandon his fallen tomato, she grew livid. *Pick that up, idiot!* In Greece, where she was born, her family never, ever wasted food, especially farm-fresh tomatoes—an essential ingredient for all the best sauces.

Her eyes narrowed as they scrutinized the thin, mustached man in a flashy sports outfit racing across the marketplace.

She glanced at the woman, whose blond head was stuffed in a plant. *La pauvre. I hope she's not his wife...*

As usual, Sylvie was wearing her favorite tie-dyed rainbow T-shirt, khaki shorts, and sandals. Unlike the majority of Belgians, Sylvie—a transplant from Santorini, Greece—couldn't care less if her shirt wasn't ironed to perfection.

Walking around smoothens out the wrinkles, she always told herself. *Especially when it drizzles.* She had the same nonchalant attitude toward makeup. *Why clog my pores just to please others?* She preferred the attitude of Yaya, her grandma: "Natural beauty is more than enough to make a woman glow." This made her grateful to wake up each day and run her fingers over her smooth skin, which—to the envy of her Belgian students—remained naturally tanned, year-round.

Leaning against the tree, Sylvie understood that she shared something special with the blond woman she was spying on, whose head was still stuffed in a plant: a passion for flowers. Each Saturday, even in terrible downpours, she ventured to the farmer's market to fetch her weekly bouquets. Friends visiting Sylvie's apartment teased her; not only were the walls as yellow as tennis balls, but colorful flowers multiplied each week.

Sylvie peered around the tree again. *Enfin!* The guy with a temper had disappeared. Her eyes fell on his girlfriend. Curiously, Sylvie felt drawn to her. The woman seemed friendly enough, and she was certainly enjoying her orange flowers. *What a contrast with Monsieur Tomato-loser.*

Sylvie emerged from behind the tree just as Hélène lifted her head. The young, dark-haired woman stepped forward, flashing her *objet d'attention* a warm, inviting smile.

❖

Hélène gasped inwardly. As if in a dream, a Greek goddess with a prominent nose, just like the ones in her high school history books, stood inches from her face. When Hélène jerked her head back, a flicker of light from the woman's eyes seared her soul. Those dark eyes—intense and rich, like chocolate.

Hélène's throat went dry. As if in a dream, she felt her body sweep in a whirlwind to the deserts of ancient Greece. A soft, sandy wind blew around her neck, caressing her skin. Just as her mind went numb, something inside her body cracked. The goddess's eyes were mesmerizing. And her full yet delicate lips…Hélène felt a tug in her stomach. When she struggled to return the smile, to her horror, a ticking sensation engulfed her entire left cheek. It began with slow movements, progressing rapidly, denting the inner walls of her face.

Hélène often developed tics in her eyes, especially after long days translating at the computer. But she had never experienced a tic like this, mid-cheek. Lacking a more suitable alternative, she stuffed her head back into the plant, vowing to lay low until the goddess left or the tic wore itself out—whichever came first.

❖

Quelle réaction bizarre. All I did was smile. Sylvie approached the plant and separated its broad, dark leaves. A pair of glasses gleamed back at her. *Hmm. Pretty eyes,* she decided, admiring the moist blue irises blinking behind thick lenses.

Sylvie spoke into the plant. *"Excusez-moi."*

Instantly, the leaves shook.

Sylvie recognized a frightened bird when she saw one. *I don't want to scare this poor woman. She's already got her hands full with that testosterone-loaded guy.*

She softened her voice. "*Excusez-moi.* Are you going to buy this plant?"

❖

Mon Dieu! She's speaking to me. Hélène tried to conceal her ticking cheek behind the foliage.

Sylvie spoke in a sugary tone as if coaxing a toddler out of her tree house. "If you're not going to buy it, I will. I just adore these flowers."

Hélène gulped. *I can't keep hiding in this plant forever, especially if she's taking it home.* Mustering up her courage, she extracted her head from the leaves. She thought she saw a halo hovering over the goddess's head. *I've got to clean these more often,* she mused, fingering her glasses. "*Vous avez raison,* they're magnificent," she stammered, sticking her nose into a tuft of orange petals. Their sweet aroma made her giddy, prompting her to forget the nasty tic in her cheek.

❖

Sylvie chuckled. *She sure is one bizarre biscuit. Guess I would be too if I had a boyfriend like that. Some people should just stay single.*

An identical plant nearby caught her eye.

"*Regardez,* here's another one," she announced. But the woman was already hauling her plant toward the cash register. Sylvie grabbed the other plant. *Mince, this bulky thing must weigh twenty kilos.* She donned her yellow army backpack, bursting with groceries, and struggled toward the cash register. She tried to keep her balance, but her backpack—with tufts of celery dangling from its faded side pockets—had other ideas. As soon as she reached the cash register, she let out an

"Aaaiieee!" and toppled over backward, straight into Hélène's arms.

❖

Like a surfer lugging her board through the waves, Hélène raced her plant toward the register. She blinked to keep the leaves out of her eyelashes as she ran; they tickled her face, and some entered her nose, but she didn't care. *Sooner I'm out of here, the better.*

There was a shuffle behind her. Next, she heard a loud "Aaaiieee!"

Before she knew it, Hélène's arms encircled the Greek goddess's waist. Grunting like a sailor, she righted the young woman. Thick, green branches dug into Hélène's ribs, but she didn't mind. She held on tight.

CHAPTER TWO

It began with her olfactory system. Hélène's nose noticed a subtle yet delightful scent emanating from the Greek goddess. *Is it her hair? Or her skin?* Something about this striking woman inspired images of all the exotic trips Hélène had planned but never took. As a child, she had dreamed of voyages to faraway islands, tropical paradises—places where she would do nothing but lie on the beach and stuff herself silly with lavish dishes bursting with forbidden spices.

Forbidden...Hélène's mind lingered on the word. With her hands clenching the goddess and her nose burrowed in her soft hair, a sea of foreign sensations swept through Hélène's body, invading it like a tidal wave, sweeping away all that wasn't secured. Hélène struggled to keep her feet firmly on the ground.

Then a burst of warm air caressed her cheek.

"*Merci,*" uttered the goddess, whose shiny lips were millimeters from Hélène's.

"No problem!" exclaimed Hélène, awkwardly removing her hands from Sylvie's waist. "You're sure loaded down," she added, trying to sound casual.

"At least I've got a car." Sylvie took off her heavy backpack.

"*Allez-y*, go ahead," said Hélène, lugging her plant behind Sylvie. "I'm not in a hurry." She winced at her quivering voice. *I'm such a bad liar.*

"If you insist." Sylvie moved her plant in front of the cash register.

"That'll be fifteen euros, *Mademoiselle*," said the florist, a sturdy man with tiny round glasses. Sylvie fumbled in her backpack. As she pulled out her surfer's wallet, her keys dropped to the ground. She turned to the blond woman. "*Au revoir.*"

"*Au revoir*," replied Hélène, blushing as the Greek goddess marched off with her plant. Like a camera, her mind recorded Sylvie's athletic silhouette. The woman's youthful body radiated excellent health, with an intriguing blend of feminine and androgynous traits. Her slim waist and broad shoulders created a unique impression on Hélène, who wished she could have said something more to her. *But what?* she wondered, watching the young woman's nimble legs stretch across the cobblestones before disappearing into the crowd.

"That'll be fifteen euros for you too, *Madame*."

Hélène hardly heard the florist. Her mind was still in overdrive. "*Eh bien.*" She glanced at her plant. *Right. I'm buying a plant.* "How often should I water it?" she blurted as she handed him the money.

"*Voyons.* How often do you take a shower, *Madame*?" The florist chuckled so hard he grabbed his chest. Normally, Hélène made an effort to laugh at his remarks. Today, she stared blankly at him.

"About half as often, *d'accord*?"

"Thanks." Hélène took a step but stopped when she saw a shiny object nestled in the synthetic grass at her feet.

"*Excusez-moi.* Is this yours?" She held up a silver

keychain in the form of a fish, with the word "Greece" etched into it. Several keys hung from its metal ring.

"Hmmm." The florist scratched his balding head. "Never seen it before. Might be your friend's."

"What friend?"

"The one who was just here with you."

The Greek goddess? Hélène stammered, "I...I don't know her."

"*C'est bizarre.* You sure seemed like friends. She's here every Saturday, just like you."

Hélène's heart thumped. "*Ah bon?*" she replied, clutching the keys.

"I was certain you knew each other. Anyway, it doesn't matter. Just give me the keys. She'll come back for them sooner or later."

Hélène contemplated the florist's outstretched palm, which resembled an heirloom tomato, with deep ridges and reddish, calloused skin.

Then she heard a tiny voice whisper: *Keep them.*

"*Non,*" she stammered. "I'll...I'll go find her. She can't have gotten very far."

The florist looked at her quizzically as she lugged her plant away.

Hélène elbowed her way through the crowds. *I've got to find her.*

Twenty minutes later, after checking all the stands, she stopped to catch her breath. Squinting, she inspected the silver fish's worn edges. *This thing is ancient. Wonder how long she's had it?* She flipped it over. A few words were engraved on the back. *It's in Greek!*

After wandering aimlessly around the market, Hélène finally gave up. She headed back to the florist's stand. But when she got there, her face fell. All that was left was an empty concrete space. She glanced at her watch. *Ah non, Marc's going to kill me!*

Just then, Hélène did something she never, ever did. She had always loathed exercise, even in school. Not only was she the slowest runner, she couldn't throw, hit, or kick a ball. Due to her uncoordinated efforts, the kids christened her *Hélène la Boulette*, which translated to *Chunky Hunky Hélène* in English. Not surprisingly, she always concocted clever excuses to escape *éducation physique* classes. Today, however, Chunky Hunky Hélène grabbed her hefty plant and, huffing and puffing, dripping and slipping, ran, ran, ran as fast as her chunky legs could carry her.

❖

When Hélène's boots finally skidded to a stop at Marc's table, her face had taken on the features of a frenzied dog. Pursing her lips to hide her frothing saliva, she thrust her hand over her pounding heart.

Hélène's dramatic arrival amused the café locals relaxing outside, sipping espressos or Belgian beers, and munching on *frites* and mayonnaise. Conversations paused when Marc, crouched at a small table littered with empty Stella Artois beer bottles, sat up, erect as a pencil. His pupils shrank to pinpoints as his eyes drilled into his wife's.

Marc's eyes reminded Hélène of a feverish monkey she had once seen at the Antwerp zoo. She took a step back as her plant hit the ground.

"*C'est pas possible, Hélène!* I've been waiting for at least an hour!"

Hélène collapsed into a plastic chair and wiped the sweat off her face. Marc leaned forward. The pilsner beers had reddened his eyes and soured his breath. His angry eyes zoomed in on his wife's precious plant. He shook the trunk violently as if to strangle it.

Hélène shuddered as orange flowers flew past her nose. *Glad that's not my neck.*

"How much did this pile of weeds cost?" hissed Marc, flinging bits of shrubbery onto nearby tables, to the coffee sippers' delight. Ignoring him, Hélène salvaged the discarded bits at her feet. Before Marc could make more of a scene, a young waiter appeared. He had bushy eyebrows, black eyes, platinum hair, and a tiny bone pierced through his left ear.

"What can I get you, *Madame?*" he asked with a slight foreign accent.

"*Un grand café au lait,*" replied Hélène, arranging the flowers in a neat pile. "And a croissant with jam and butter, *s'il vous plaît.*"

"We just had breakfast!" protested Marc, downing his beer.

Hélène peered at the lifeless flowers on their table. Stifling her anger, she blurted, "It's Saturday. Might as well live it up!"

"*D'accord.* Let's celebrate, then." Marc rose and swaggered into the café. "I'll start by taking a piss."

Instead of soaking up her husband's insults, Hélène purged them from her thoughts. She took out the silver "Greece" fish keychain and fingered its strange inscription. *Wish I could read this.* The silvery fish, resting on her pile of discarded flowers, shimmered in the sunlight. *Just like a holy shrine*, she mused. *But in honor of whom?* Hélène's eyes scanned the marketplace. The crowds had thinned. She felt her cheek twitching again. *How can I find her?*

Sneakered feet shuffled behind Hélène as the waiter appeared with her breakfast. He swept aside the pile of flowers and set down the tray.

"*Tiens*, I've got one just like this!" he exclaimed, grabbing the shiny keychain.

"*M'enfin!* What the heck are you doing?" Hélène jumped up. "Give that back at once!"

Ignoring her, the waiter squinted to read the worn Greek letters.

"'To my dearest Joanna, with all my love forever. Théodoros.'" He cocked a pierced eyebrow at Hélène.

"You speak Greek?" she asked, surprised.

"Ain't Yiddish, *Madame*. I'm imported. Direct from the islands. Don't tell me you're Joanna?"

Hélène gave him a blank look as she contemplated the words "With all my love forever." *Wonder who wrote that? Who's Théodoros?*

The waiter dangled the silver fish in front of her. "*Alors*, are you Joanna or—" he began in Greek.

"I said give it back! It's my friend's." As Hélène snatched the keychain, her elbow hit something hard.

"*Putain!*" yelled Marc, clutching his ribs. Stella Artois suds flooded the pile of flowers. He swiped the shiny keychain from Hélène's fingers.

"*Alors*, who's your friend?" he demanded, dangling it before Hélène's nose.

"Ah, nobody. I found it."

Marc cleared his throat. "And I'm Father Christmas."

"*Vraiment, chéri.*" Hélène grimaced at her café-drenched croissant. "I found it at the—"

"I'm not deaf, Hélène," hissed Marc. "You *said* it was your friend's!"

Hélène leaned away to escape her husband's brewery breath.

"So who's this friend of yours?"

"I told you. I found it at the flower—" Then something colorful caught her eye. "*Ah!*" she squealed. Her stomach grew queasy. The Greek goddess in a tie-dyed T-shirt was standing before their table, beaming at her.

"*Super!* I've been looking all over for that!" gushed Sylvie.

Marc looked at the young woman in shorts, then at his wife, and back at the young woman. While his neck was busy swiveling, Hélène snatched the keys from him. She opened her mouth, but nothing came out. All she could do was keep from swallowing her tongue.

"*Je...*" she stammered, avoiding Sylvie's glossy brown eyes to focus on the younger woman's muscular thighs. Underneath her khaki shorts, tiny blond hairs grazed their smooth, tan surface. *How could these be blond if she's Greek? My legs are as white as aspirin and as flabby as...* She gulped. *I'd die for a pair of legs like these.*

Sylvie's voice interrupted her thoughts.

"When I saw the florist was gone, I flipped. But I had a hunch I might find you here. And I was right! I can't tell you how relieved I am."

Hélène clenched the keys in a futile attempt to control her facial muscles. The tic was making its rounds again. She tilted her head sideways.

"I...I looked everywhere but couldn't find you," Hélène stammered, forcing a diagonal smile at the beaming goddess. She thrust out her hand. "*Voilà.*"

Sylvie lifted the keys from her sweaty palm.

"How sweet of you. I'm so relieved!"

Hélène nodded. "I bet you are. You couldn't go home without them."

"*Comment?* The keys? I couldn't care less about those."

The goddess chuckled. "My car's a junker. *This* is what I was worried about." Sylvie held up the silver fish with "Greece" written on it. She hugged it to her chest. "I'd die if I lost it!"

Hélène heard a snicker. Directly behind the goddess stood the waiter. *He's ogling the goddess. Makes sense. She's stunning.* Then Hélène remembered his words as he read the Greek message on the keychain: *With all my love forever.* Inexplicably, she started to feel queasy.

❖

Sylvie could feel his eyes on her body. She could always tell when guys were checking her out, even from behind. It made her skin crawl. *I should have put on the Bermudas.*

After the waiter had fully examined Sylvie's firm backside and shapely calves, he addressed her in Greek. "Hey, Joanna..." When she didn't respond, he tried, "Joanna, my sweetheart..."

Sylvie pretended she couldn't hear him as she gazed at the woman who had found her keys. She tried to ignore the stream of negative thoughts running through her mind: *I'm so sick of guys. They're such scavengers, scrounging around for a tasty morsel of anything female.* She averted her eyes from the man whose eyes were red from drinking. He seemed to be glowering at her. *This jerk wins the prize.* She flashed an apologetic smile at the woman.

"*Eh bien,* I've got to go. *Merci encore. Kalí óreksi!*" Sylvie said, skirting past the waiter before he could call her any more ridiculous names.

❖

Hélène watched the goddess's nimble figure skip over the cobblestones despite her grocery-laden backpack. *She can't be real.* When she shut her eyes, time skidded to a stop. Yet her heart continued to beat, furiously, like a powerful African drum. A mysterious force drew her in as her mind went into a trance. Matching the tam-tam beat, her chest's jerky movements swelled, inflating her blouse. A tender spot surfaced beneath her heart. Through her soft pink eyelids, she saw an oblong blob. It turned into a tree—a familiar tree, a hollow tree. She understood the message: *I am the tree.*

Hélène's body quivered in the midst of a flourishing grove, squeezing back the tears, braving the elements, camouflaging her emptiness. A gust of wind erupted. Her outer crust—the bark of her soul—scraped against her skin, like flimsy plywood flapping at a timeworn façade. Her roots, dry as ashes, had forgotten their purpose in life—to soak nutrients from the soil.

C'est ça. I've hit rock bottom. That's why I feel all flaky and rotten inside. She could feel her body struggling to face the world. *I'm a limp twig. And I can't even float.* A shiver ran down her spine.

Whenever Hélène felt the truth, the raw truth, about something important, her spine would tingle, like someone flipped a switch. Sparks of electricity would rip from the nape of her neck through the soles of her feet, toward the core of the earth.

Hélène's eyes snapped open. Her face was still tingling. She had never seen that Greek woman before, but somehow she seemed so familiar. She watched her glide over the cobblestones like a potato chip floating in the wind. *That's it— she's my exact opposite. I'm heavy and bland; she's light and flavorful. I'm a lump, and she's a goddess.*

Just then, as if the goddess had heard Hélène's thoughts,

she turned and waved. Hélène wiggled her fingers timidly at the tiny figure on the horizon.

As soon as the goddess was out of sight, Hélène took a bite from her soggy croissant.

A gruff voice jolted her from her reverie. "Who the heck was that?"

Hélène swallowed. "Nobody."

Marc's eyes narrowed. "What do you mean, nobody? You seem to—"

"Name's Joanna," cut in the waiter as he removed Marc's empty beer glasses.

Hélène glared at the young man and flashed a coy look at her husband.

"*Pardon, chéri.* Did I forget to introduce you?"

CHAPTER THREE

It had been ten painful years. Ever since Maman had died, Hélène could no longer pick up the phone to release her troubles. She missed their long, intimate phone calls and endless chats over steamy cups of café au lait in Maman's kitchen. Only flowers could comfort her now, drowning out these absurd scientific translations. Buried under piles of botany books, Hélène thrived in this secret world of poetry. Her innocent, flowery prose soothed her soul.

She had been writing her poems for years, yet she shared them with no one, and certainly not with Marc. She had a few friends but was more of a listener than a reciter of wants and woes. To make up for this, Hélène resorted to flower worship and clandestine poem dedications to exalt their beauty. This was her only real source of happiness in life, along with Chaussette, her dear cat.

Hélène chewed on another cookie as she perused her latest literary creation at work. She whispered as she read her latest poem: "The flower, a poem in itself, hides behind the dark, tangled leaves of life. It remains shy about who it is, never truly revealing itself but for great, unexpected moments. It envies the butterfly, free to roam…"

I'm no Keats, d'accord, but still… Hélène focused her

attention on her orange flowers, whose wrinkly petals were finally perking up after their cramped journey in her purse. Suddenly, her eyes blurred. The yo-yo became a go-go as the petals danced before her eyes. The petals' circular swirls hypnotized Hélène while her mind drifted back to the market café.

The Greek goddess was standing before her, hugging her keychain to her chest. "I'd die if I lost it!" she exclaimed, smiling warmly at Hélène.

The pitter-patter of footsteps in the hall roused Hélène from her daydream. Monsieur Lamie, Hélène's pudgy boss, poked the tip of his waxy mustache into her office. Hélène's nostrils sensed the familiar odor of old cigars and cheap toilet water. Swiftly, she switched screens. The aphid text, which she was supposed to be working on, popped up again. Hunching over her keyboard, she pretended to translate; her fingers churned out a strange concoction: "xjioptezomqhtoeirupqkm jkeopqthqmlsdtjçszem…"

This charade always satisfied Monsieur Lamie, whose chunky glasses wore a perpetual coat of mustache wax and dust. He trusted his ears; as soon as he heard Hélène's fingers tapping the keys, his handlebar mustache folded upward, and he tiptoed away.

Hélène cast a look behind her to make sure he was gone. Relieved, she bit into another cookie and sipped her coffee. *Hmm, bitter.* After dumping in a sixth packet of sugar, she switched screens to work on her precious poem.

"It envies the butterfly, free to roam," she repeated. As Hélène savored her syrupy coffee, her eyelids drooped. The caffeine wasn't doing its trick this morning.

"How timely!" She yawned at a butterfly fluttering outside. The rapid movements of its yellow wings mesmerized her. Before she could stop herself, her yellow hair spilled over the keyboard, and she succumbed to the pleasures of temporary mental hibernation.

❖

Hélène lifted her groggy head from her desk. *I need some air*, she decided, wrenching herself from her chair. In the ladies' room, she ran an enormous pink brush through her mousy hair. She frowned at her mirrored image. As a child, the neighborhood kids had called her "dishwater Hélène," her hair was so lifeless. Even now, despite dozens of daily strokes, her blond mop looked like it had gone through extensive dishwashing cycles. *Some things never change.*

Hélène searched her blue eyes for hints of liveliness. But all she saw was boredom. Removing her glasses, she squinted at the blurry face in the mirror. *Time for our weapons.*

She applied some foundation, then rouge, with a large fluffy brush. Powder flew into the air. She sneezed. Cocking back her head, she inserted a tube of nose drops into her nostrils and inhaled deeply. Next, she dabbed concealer under her eyes. Then she applied a sea of sparkly blue eye shadow. Cranking her mouth open, she lined her lids with teal blue, then topped them off with sticky black mascara.

Hélène's routine in the ladies' room never faltered. Twice a day, for the past twenty years, she had painted her face and brushed her hair in exactly the same fashion, always finishing her masterpiece with cherry lipstick.

She donned her glasses and scrunched her nose. *I look better blurry.*

❖

The next afternoon, a smile lingered on Hélène's lips. In her daydream, she had been wandering the beach on a tropical island, trying to make sense of her life. She could still feel the sand between her toes and the salty breeze in her hair. She glanced at her office clock. It was 4:15.

Time sure flies when you're working hard. She chortled. *But it's not my fault. This scientific stuff is so dry...*

She rubbed imaginary sand from her eyes and sipped her coffee. The cold, sugary liquid tickled her throat. She sneezed. With a quick snap of the head, she inserted her allergy drops.

Just as she began translating again, the phone rang.

"Hélène? *C'est moi.* Listen...Maman's just flown in from Spain, so I've invited her for dinner. I'm on my way to the airport. *Chérie,* can you concoct something she won't detest for a change? A good roast, or perhaps a..."

This is all I need. Hélène's skin crawled at the idea of another dinner with Marc's mother. How she hated her impromptu visits to their home. Her heart beat faster. She felt the blood pumping in her ears while the room began to spin.

❖

Cecile Beaucils took her usual rounds during her afternoon *pause café.* After filling her mug with milky decaf, she headed straight to Hélène's office. Not only was Cecile incontestably the most attractive secretary in the marketing department, she was Hélène's best friend. As soon as Cecile saw Hélène—who was usually gazing out the window or typing frenetically at her keyboard—she gasped. Her best friend lay unconscious on the floor, legs splayed, with her telephone dangling from her desk.

Unceremoniously, Cecile stooped in her silk miniskirt and shook her friend's shoulders.

"Hélène? Hélène! *Ca va?* Help, somebody! Help!"

CHAPTER FOUR

Sylvie Routard sat on her balcony outside her fourth-floor apartment. Light from the moon fused with the soft rays of a tiny lamp above her head, illuminating Sylvie and the plants thriving on her balcony. She wore her usual garb—denim shorts and a yellow T-shirt. There was nothing she would rather do than spend a quiet evening reading a good novel outdoors.

But she wasn't alone in the cool summer breeze. As usual, she indulged in the warmth of Goldie, her orange cat, curled up in her lap. Evenings like this meant pure pleasure. Savoring her owner's infinite caresses, Goldie purred while Sylvie hummed, creating a unique melody to enhance the soft Greek music emanating from the living room.

Sylvie reached for her Greek cocktail. When Goldie hopped off her lap, her bushy tail knocked off an orange flower. Sylvie stopped humming.

"Look what you did to our new plant!" She brought the severed flower to her nose, inhaling its sugary nectar. Then she plopped the flower into her Greek cocktail and brought her glass to her lips. Peering at the silvery moon, she started humming again.

Surrounded by so many plants, she felt like Jane of the Jungle, although the only wild animal in her midst was Goldie, purring at her bare feet. Suddenly, she felt an unexpected surge of energy. As she swayed her muscular hips, the impromptu nocturnal dance made her cat purr even harder. A tiny stream of cocktail landed on the ground. Before Sylvie could stop her, Goldie lapped it up.

"And I thought I was the wild one!" exclaimed Sylvie.

❖

Sylvie sat with her sneakered feet dangling over a bar stool at her neighborhood hangout, Dionysos Taverna. Her white T-shirt and worn blue jeans blended into the Greek restaurant's faded blue and whitewashed walls. A dark-haired waiter stood nearby, watching her contemplate where to next poke her fork. She was hesitating between three succulent dishes.

"This is so intense!" she exclaimed in Greek, inserting another forkful of eggplant soufflé into her mouth. She closed her eyes as her tongue detected the familiar spices from Santorini that rendered these dishes so special. *Mmm... cinnamon.* Her eyeballs rolled in their sockets.

"You're exaggerating, *i kopela mou.*" The olive-skinned waiter blew circles of smoke from his cigarette into her hair.

"Stop polluting my air, Vassilios," scolded Sylvie. "You're ruining my appetite."

"Come on, Syl. It would take a forest fire to separate you from your dinner. And that's only if it started burning your luscious hair." The waiter tapped Sylvie playfully on the shoulder. Sylvie tapped him back, harder.

"All right, you win." Rubbing his rugged shoulder, the waiter stubbed out his cigarette and lifted his retsina wine.

Clinking her glass against his, Sylvie parted her lips,

inviting the chilled white nectar of her homeland into her mouth.

❖

Sylvie's eyes snapped open. Orange light streamed into her bedroom, dancing through the soft curtains, illuminating her bed. She grabbed her cat from her perch and hugged her to her pajamas. "*Mon petit chou!*"

Sylvie tied back her hair, threw on a sweatshirt, and jogged down the stairs of her apartment building. Outside, she took a whiff of fresh air and crossed the street. She was pushing on a tree trunk to stretch her Achilles tendon when a car approached with teenage boys inside. One rolled down the window.

"Push all you want, *Madame*. It ain't goin' nowhere!"

"How clever," Sylvie announced over the boys' ensuing sneers. The car sped away.

Twenty minutes later, she reached a grassy park. Catching her breath, she scanned the wide expanse of grass, dotted with tall pines and rows of freshly planted blossoms. Her heart pounded under her moist sweatshirt, matching her rapid breathing.

Belly first, she plopped on the lawn and furrowed her nose into tufts of grass.

Bet there's a four-leafer around here. She weaved her fingertips through patches of dark green clovers. The scent of dewy grass mixed with dirt filled her nostrils. As her heartbeat decelerated, her body—splayed comfortably on the grass— relaxed. Her spirit felt in tune with the world.

Voilà! She plucked a four-leaf clover from the grass, inspected it, then tucked it into her shorts pocket.

Once home, after a hot shower, she ventured out to her terrace for a well-deserved, healthy breakfast.

"Look what Maman found." She twirled the clover in front of Goldie's nose.

"We're getting lucky, *bébé!*" she announced, digging her spoon into a huge bowl of muesli.

❖

Sylvie lay upon her spacious bed with her blue-jeaned limbs sprawled open. An orange ceiling light cast a warm glow through thin paper onto her face; her eyes were peacefully shut.

Dozens of black-and-white photos surrounded her immobile, athletic silhouette, peppering the silk orange bedcover. Purring on an embroidered cushion, Goldie lay next to her mistress, paws clinging to her thick, wavy hair. Sylvie's lips softened as her ears absorbed the nearby purring mingled with her melodious Greek Gypsy music.

On evenings like this, after endless hours developing her week's photos—Sylvie spent nearly all her free time taking pictures—she loved to chill. Her mind would wander, imagining she were a bohemian with no cares in the world. As her weary muscles sank deeper into the heavenly bedspread, she wished life could always be so comfortable. A lively Gypsy song from a Greek CD freshly unearthed at the market roused Sylvie's placid thoughts. Her eyes went to the window's lacy curtains flowing in the evening breeze. Matching the song's rhythm, they spread full and collapsed, like sails adorning the ships from her native island.

With each powerful note, traces of Sylvie's ancestors entered her mind, bringing back tender memories of Santorini, her colorful neighborhood, her family…

She smiled, thinking of her beloved grandma, Yaya, who used to grasp her fingers and proclaim in her throaty Greek voice, "Soak up the pleasures in life, honey. Every little bit of 'em. Make 'em seep through your pores till you burst." She would stare into her granddaughter's innocent eyes and continue, "And never be afraid of love. When it hits, make sure you grab it with both hands. 'Cause you never know when it's going to leave you for good."

Sylvie often found herself pondering the implication of Yaya's message. In her thirty-six years, it hadn't made much sense so far. But her grandma never failed to utter it, especially on significant days like Sylvie's parents' anniversary or a birthday. Opening her weathered lips, Yaya would pronounce each sentence ever so slowly. Like a divine affirmation, she would gently lift her tongue and release her magic message.

Just then, Sylvie felt a presence as if Yaya were lying beside her. Searching for comfort, she stroked Goldie, who lifted her drowsy head. *Wonder how she's doing. Maybe I should give her a call.* The thought lingered in her mind until fatigue won out and Sylvie's eyelids folded again. Goldie snuggled up to her mistress and, within seconds, purred them both to sleep.

Chapter Five

I feel like such an idiot, thought Hélène for the fiftieth time that evening. Clad in Marc's old sports clothes and a red cycling helmet, she straddled her new bike. *Hope nobody can see me.*

Hélène began to pedal. Marc gripped her side as she carved wide circles in the parking lot.

"You're on your own," he announced, letting go. Instantly, the front wheel wobbled.

"Aaaiie!" yelped Hélène, hitting the asphalt.

"You'll be fine, *chérie*. Try again."

Hélène shook her head. "*Non*, I've had enough for today."

"But we just started."

"I feel like such a loser." *I am a loser.* "I quit."

Her thoughts flashed back to a recent difficult conversation with her doctor.

After Hélène had fainted at work, Dr. Duprès gave her a pile of medical pamphlets, instructing her to change her diet and exercise more. "Why don't you try running, cycling, or swimming—"

"I don't exactly do sports." Hélène blushed, staring at her chubby ankles, remembering how her teachers forced her to participate in gym classes. Nobody would pick her for kickball, or volleyball, or softball, she was so uncoordinated.

Dr. Duprès continued, "To start, I suggest you go walking or ride your bike, at least a half hour every day."

"Every day?" Hélène's voice had cracked.

"*Exactement.* You'll get used to it. You'll even start to like it." Dr. Duprès had smiled. "You'll have more energy too."

Hélène's thoughts returned to the parking lot as Marc pulled his wife to her feet. "Just one more time."

He held the back of her bike as she pedaled. "That's great, *chérie.* You're an athlete!"

An athlete? she thought. *More like a toddler. "Merde!"* she yelled as her body flew sideways.

After practicing unsuccessfully each morning, instead of losing weight, Hélène was losing her patience. One rainy day, however, a voice inside her head whispered, *Give it one more try.* Hélène shrugged her soggy shoulders and complied. To her surprise, she pedaled down the street without falling.

"*Regardez-moi!*" she yelled through the downpour. A feeling of triumph swept over her as tears formed in her eyes.

The voice told her: *Tomorrow, you're biking to work. And every day after that.*

Hélène squinted at the swollen clouds. *What are you trying to tell me?*

In response, a drop of rain trickled down her helmet into her eye, mingling with her salty tears. She nodded solemnly at the clouds, oblivious of how this vow would forever transform her life.

❖

The next morning, Hélène swung a leg over her bike. After a loud *rrrriiiiipppp*, she plunged toward the pavement. *Quelle idiote. Nobody bikes in a skirt.* Limping into the house, she reappeared in faded stretch pants. She pedaled slowly; each time a car passed, she veered toward the curb.

Then she spotted a figure jogging along the sidewalk.

The woman wore shorts and a white T-shirt, her dark hair bouncing over broad shoulders. Hélène gasped, recognizing the tan, muscular legs. *It's her!*

She sped. Just before she caught up with the woman, she heard *Honk! Honk!*

"Aaaiiiee!" she screamed, swerving to the right. A school bus was heading straight at her. Struggling to control her wiggly front wheel, she caught a diagonal glimpse of the white T-shirt before her body soared over the handlebars.

"*Idiote!* Trying to get yourself killed?" yelled the driver as his bus skidded past Hélène's body, sprawled on the curb.

Hélène lifted an eyelid. *What a spectacular move.* She jiggled her head, just like she did with used lightbulbs, as she cautiously mounted her bike. *Good. No broken bits.*

Her smile faded as soon as the woman in the T-shirt waved.

Mon Dieu, it's her. The goddess! Hélène cringed. *Perfect timing.*

The goddess hollered something that resembled a "*bonjour*" and continued jogging down the street.

Hélène scanned the sidewalk until the T-shirt disappeared. *I hope she didn't recognize me. I'm such a klutz.* She wiped off the sweat trickling down her face. *Wonder what they'll think of me at the office?*

❖

Hélène ran straight into the ladies' room. The mirror made her skid to a stop. Her wet face was unbelievably red—and glowing. *I feel so alive...* Her heart pounded under her sweaty shirt as she splashed water on her face. Huge drops ran off her chin. She hobbled into a toilet stall.

When she reappeared in a baggy skirt and blouse, tiny pieces of toilet paper stuck to her face. Giggling, she freed her cheeks from the sticky bits. Then she noticed moistness under her armpits. She dug into her bag. "Nothing a few squirts can't fix," she muttered, shooting eau de cologne under each arm. She brushed her hair vigorously and touched up her makeup, ending the makeover session with bright red lipstick.

Then something made her sneeze. She inserted allergy drops into her nose. *Wonder if I'm allergic to myself?*

As Hélène was leaving the ladies' room, she ran smack into her best friend and colleague, Cecile.

"You're all red," Cecile exclaimed as they kissed each other on the cheek. "And hot!" Her fingers went to her face. "*Ca va?* Are you all right?"

Hélène flashed her pretty colleague a sweaty grin. "Guess what? I just biked all the way to work. Never felt more alive!"

"*Quelle horreur,*" Cecile exclaimed, inspecting her moist fingers. "Your exercise addiction better not be contagious."

❖

Hélène yawned at her office computer and reached into her drawer. Mechanically, she opened her mouth to insert a chocolate-chip cookie. She stopped when its sweet, chocolaty scent invaded her nostrils. Extending the tip of her tongue, her taste buds caressed the cookie. Bits of dark Belgian chocolate melted in her mouth. As she savored their bitterness, conflict came: *Non, non, non. You made a promise to Dr. Duprès. No more sweets!* Before she could dissuade herself, she threw the saliva-covered cookie into the trash.

In fact, she chucked every single cookie—like mini pastry Frisbees—into the can. The dull, clunking noises against metal gave her momentum. When she had emptied all four packages from her drawer, she leaned back with glee. But her satisfaction was short-lived.

Just when she tried to salvage a cookie from the trash, her conscience took over. Before she knew it, she was erect in the can, pounding cookies with her boots. *So this is how you make a cookie crumble!* she mused, swiveling her hips and grinding her heels.

At that moment, Cecile walked by. The two colleagues were complete mismatches, yet solid confidantes. Unlike Hélène, Cecile went to extreme efforts to enhance her petite, feminine appearance. She wore sexy, tight-fitting clothes and highlighted her dark hair with soft reddish tints.

Cecile hurried into Hélène's office, slammed the door, and observed her best friend dancing in a garbage can with a hysterical look on her face.

"*Ca ne va pas du tout.*" Cecile waved her scarf in the air. "I know you fainted the other day, but what in the heck did that doctor give you?"

Hélène's lips parted, but she was laughing so hard, only honking noises came out.

Cecile shook her head. "I hate to tell you, *ma puce*, but it looks like you've got some serious side effects to that drug." She cracked her chewing gum.

Hélène opened her mouth to reassure her, releasing a fit of giggles. She pulled Cecile into a hug as tears of childish glee rolled down her cheeks, moistening the cookie crumble at her feet.

❖

After two weeks, Hélène's efforts were finally paying off. Even now, in the middle of rush hour, she felt confident pedaling through the streets of Brussels.

I'll just check out the neighborhood on my way home. She finally stopped at a grassy spot in Parc Cinquantenaire where teenagers were doing aerobics. *I didn't know they had classes here. Where have I been all these years?* Then she saw an elderly group wearing starched white kimonos, practicing martial arts under a massive tree. They were performing slow, gracious moves with their hands.

C'est beau! Wonder what that is?

When she pedaled home, a wave of unsettling vibrations swept over her body, which was already shaking from riding over cobblestones. As the wind forced its way into her jacket, something told her these vibes stemmed from a deeper source. As they surged through her, they released physical and emotional tension stagnating inside for years.

Beaming, she filled her lungs with crisp air. She had done the unthinkable—venturing outside her comfort zone. These initial baby steps led her to unearth the world, starting with Brussels, her own city, creating a whole new field of vibrations. Without knowing it, instead of simply "turning over a new leaf," her baby steps would become leaps. If she saw what was down the bumpy road, however, she would realize these vibrations were growing stronger, priming the soil and embedding the seeds for a radically new life.

❖

As she was riding home the next evening, Hélène came across a sign blocking her usual route. Following the detour signs, she entered an unfamiliar tree-lined street. Halfway down, she rode past a building displaying a large banner advertising "Swimming Lessons."

She muttered under her breath, *who needs swimming lessons?* Then it hit her. *Maybe I do?* She did a U-turn. The sign read: "Piscine Palace: private swimming lessons for adults. Give us a call!" She jotted down the phone number.

Once home, she downed two glasses of water and announced to Chaussette, "Guess what Maman's going to do, *bébé?*"

Before she could stop herself, Hélène grabbed the phone. "*Bonsoir.* Piscine Palace?"

The man on the other end embarked on a long-winded tirade extolling the virtues of learning to swim, specifically as an adult. But Hélène hardly listened. As soon as he said the word "pool," her mind gravitated to her childhood, when she systematically cried at the poolside to escape going into the water. The last-ditch antics usually worked. Ever since she was little, she'd been terrified of pools, swimming lessons, and drowning.

As the man continued, Hélène looked at her fingers grasping the phone. Those couldn't be hers. *There really must be two of me.* The real Hélène would never, ever call this number and ask for torture. She was on the verge of apologizing and hanging up when the man said, "It's never too late."

That's just what Dr. Duprès said.

She remembered sitting alone on the beach, watching her classmates race each other into the frothy waves. She had felt so lonely during that high school field trip to Ostende on the Belgian coast. She was the only one in her class who couldn't swim.

Without quite realizing how it happened, Hélène agreed to private swimming lessons at seven o'clock every morning.

"One last thing...When do I start?" She gasped. "Tomorrow?"

Hélène's legs were tingling by the time she hung up. "What do you think of that, Chaussette?" she purred, prancing around with the feline cradled in her arms. "Maman's going to learn to swim! Like a fishy, fishy, fishy..." she sang, then stopped abruptly.

"Maman doesn't even have a bathing suit! *Mon Dieu!* And the stores are going to close!" Whisking the cat to the floor, she snatched her purse and scurried toward the garage.

CHAPTER SIX

S ylvie did her best to keep her sneakers on flat surfaces as she jogged through the capital's bustling streets. This was not an easy feat, with summer roadwork and throngs of schoolkids cramming the sidewalks. When she reached Avenue des Nerviens, she felt better. No more whizzing cars. In Parc Cinquantenaire, she ran straight to a grassy spot, flinging herself under her favorite pine tree. Breathing hard, she spread her legs in a futile attempt to grasp her toes.

She knew she would never be as flexible as a gymnast. An ex had told her that her body was 80 percent swimmer, 20 percent jogger, and 0 percent gymnast. Her ex was right. Certain movements, like this one, made no sense. But she knew how sore she would be if she didn't stretch. *Only five kilometers, but still...*

She pushed her nose at the ground, relaxing into the challenge as the moist odor of tender grass hit her nostrils. She held her breath at the sight of a ladybug balancing on a tip of grass, contemplating its glossy red and black form. Ladybugs had always reminded Sylvie of her grandmother: remarkable, yet vulnerable.

Ever so gently, she blew her breath on the critter.

A gruff voice interrupted her bliss. "I knew I'd find you here."

Sylvie's heart sank. *Ah non, not again.* She ignored the voice and kept on blowing.

"*Alors*, still trying to be Superwoman? Or is it Superjock?"

Sylvie's back muscles tightened. Moistness trickled under her arms. Before she could straighten, she knew she was cornered.

"You won't mind if I join you," ordered the voice. A blond woman with a synthetic smile and dangling gold earrings threw down a newspaper, which landed a foot from Sylvie's head.

Attempting to kneel in her Chanel suit and sheer stockings, the woman grimaced at the sound of ripping nylon. "*Merde!*"

Sylvie swung her legs together. "*En fait*, I was just on my way—"

"Come on, *mon lapin*, I saw you. You just got here. Hard to miss all that huffing and puffing. And you're sweating up a lake." The woman's eyes bored into Sylvie's.

"Isn't it a bit late to find out you can't hide things from Lydia?" The blond woman placed her hand firmly on Sylvie's shoulder. Digging her long, silver fingernails into the androgynous woman's T-shirt, she forced her to stay put.

"So you've been spying on me again." Crossing her legs, Sylvie glared at her impromptu visitor.

Lydia laughed nervously. "You wish!" She scanned the grass. "I just happened to be taking a walk in the—"

"*D'accord*, Lydia. You just happened to drive thirty kilometers in rush-hour traffic to come take a stroll in my neighborhood park at eight a.m. on a Tuesday morning."

Lydia dug her fingernails deeper into Sylvie's skin. "First of all, it's not your park. It's a public space. It belongs to everyone."

"*D'accord.*" Sylvie shook the woman's hand off her

shoulder. "But you just happen to live in Flanders, where you have so many beaut—"

"Cut the crap. Why didn't you return my calls?" The Chanel woman's eyes were glistening.

Sylvie clenched her jaw. *I will not let her do this to me. Not again.*

Lydia's voice quivered. "We agreed we'd be friends. But it's been four months, and no word from you at all." Feigning a frown, she plucked a few blades of grass. "You never answer your phone. You never seem to be at work."

Sylvie's nostrils flared. "I can't take phone calls while I'm working. You know that."

"If you can call what you do 'working.'" Lydia rolled her eyes.

Sylvie glared at her. "*Ah non*, not this again. We're not going there."

"Never mind. I...I was worried about you. I was afraid you did something drastic, like leave Belgium for good, or something." Lydia's voice cracked.

"I would've told you," said Sylvie, softening her voice.

"But what if something happened to me? What if I got sick, like really sick? I could've died, and you—" Like a Broadway actress, Lydia brushed off imaginary tears with the back of her wrist.

"You're a strong woman, Lydia."

"But you don't care anymore, *n'est-ce pas*? You never cared!" Lydia pouted.

Sylvie inhaled deeply to steady herself. "We agreed it was over. Remember?"

"But I trusted you, Sylvie," burst Lydia, ripping up bits of grass around her knees.

The way she whined reminded Sylvie of a spoiled child

fussing over spilled ice cream. *So obnoxious.* Sylvie felt her ears grow hot as her temper rose. "You trusted *me*? What's this? You go off on one of your fancy business trips and you—" Her voice broke off.

"But it only happened once, and I did apologize."

"We're not going to go over this again, Lydia. It's time to move on." Sylvie could feel the sore spot in her chest, a mental bruise from the past, stabbing at her heart. "*De toute façon*, in case you forgot, you're a happily married woman," she retorted with a sneer.

"That's not fair! Leave him out of this."

Sylvie rose and, after a few brisk arm swings, announced firmly, "*Désolée*, Lydia. This time, it really is over." She held up her sports watch. "And it's time for me to run."

Still perched pristinely on her newspaper, Lydia struggled to untangle her legs. "*Mon lapin*, wait!" But before she could move, a curt "*ciao*" answered her plea. As Chanel woman watched a certain white T-shirt zoom away, her former lover's carefree attitude created havoc with her system. Her lipstick-drenched lips tightened into a scowl that she would most likely wear for the remainder of the day.

❖

That evening, soft red light cast a mysterious hue over Sylvie's face as she lifted the last photo. With rubber tongs, she shook the black-and-white print paper. A few drops of chemicals dropped back into the tray. With the skill of a seasoned developer, she hung the wet photo next to the others suspended on a string in the improvised darkroom in her bathroom. A timer clicked in the corner, counting the seconds before Sylvie had to transfer her next batch of photos.

She relished these moments in the evening when her sole

task was to obey the timer. In the quiet darkness, her thoughts came to a standstill. These precious pauses in life let her concentrate on nothing but her art.

Tonight, she hardly noticed the fatigue in her legs from her morning five-kilometer run. She stood firmly in her running shoes, her muscles obscured by the darkroom's blackness. She hummed as she squinted at the photo dangling above her head. She could barely make out the black forms on its glossy white surface.

She drew closer to inspect the image's contours. *Needs more contrast. I should have used filter number four.* The timer buzzed. As she extracted the first photo from her new batch, she stopped humming when she heard a familiar ring tone. She glanced at her backpack on the stool. *Great timing, Lydia.* She continued hanging the wet photos while her cell phone played its music, her neck muscles stiffening as the sounds droned on. When she finally reached for her backpack, the music stopped. *Great timing*, she repeated to herself, slumping against the wall.

Later that evening, Sylvie's home phone rang. After two rings, she threw down her napkin. *This is getting old.* Lettuce-and-turkey sandwich in hand, she checked the number displayed.

"*Ah, bonsoir*, Monsieur Lasalle…You called me earlier?" She pulled on a strand of hair as she listened to her boss. "Afraid of what? Don't worry, I'll take care of it."

She hung up the phone. "Looks like we'll be getting up early for a while, Goldie." She handed a bit of turkey to her cat. "And I guess I'll have to start jogging in the evenings."

Sylvie pondered the thought while watching Goldie lick her paws. Then she chuckled. "At least that'll keep Lydia off our backs for a couple of weeks!"

CHAPTER SEVEN

*E*verything seems so different in the dark, Hélène realized, inhaling the scent of fresh rain from the night. All was silent except for an occasional plane and the brittle sound of gravel crunching under her tires. Her bike light shone weakly on the ground as she rode through the slick streets.

Hélène was struggling to maintain her balance, and right before she reached the pool, she heard heavy wheels skidding on the pavement. A truck whizzed past her. The driver honked, causing her to swerve to the curb. *C'est super dangereux!* Hélène realized, slamming on her brakes. She vowed to buy one of those ugly fluorescent cycling vests.

The last thing I need is to get hit by one of these mad drivers before my first private swimming lesson. Dr. Duprès told me I had to exercise to reduce my cholesterol levels, but riding around Brussels at the crack of dawn every morning might be overdoing it.

❖

After Hélène's third set of knocks on the heavy wooden door, and still no answer, she nudged it open. The lights were on. "*Bonjour,*" she called out, peering inside.

Already 6:50. Might as well go in.

Halfway down the hall, Hélène entered an empty room. The faint odor of fresh paint and disinfectant roused her nostrils. After glancing at the shiny pink and green walls, her eyes fell on a pair of turbo hair dryers.

Must be the locker room. She popped behind a blue plastic shower curtain adorned with baby fish. Reappearing in her new bathing suit and swim cap after an impromptu shopping spree, she shuddered at her reflection in the mirror. The fluorescent lights made her body glow. *White as aspirin.* Quickly covering herself with a towel, she entered a bathroom stall.

Just as she started to sit down, she heard footsteps in the locker room. There was a jingling of keys, then a light thump. Next, she heard a rustling shower curtain. She began to sweat. *Sure hope I'm in the women's.* This thought made her lose the urge; she tiptoed out of the stall.

At least I've got some color now, she mused, staring at her flushed face in the mirror. *But this swim cap is hideous.* As she was tucking in her blond locks, something shiny on the counter caught her eyes.

It was a keychain sporting a silver fish with the word "Greece" etched into it, exactly like the one she had found weeks before. Before Hélène could react, she heard rustling sounds behind her. *Now or never!* She tiptoed over to a shower curtain, took a gulp of air, and peeked underneath. All she could see were two tan ankles. One of them was wearing a colorful bead anklet. Then she lifted her eyes. Attached to the ankles were two muscular calves. Hélène felt a rush of adrenaline. Behind the calves, she spotted an old yellow backpack. *Ah, non!* Five tan toes inserted themselves into a yellow and green flip-flop. Then five more toes...

Trying to outrace her pounding heart, Hélène scrambled

out of the locker room before the flip-flops could catch up with her.

❖

Hélène had no idea where she was headed, but her bare feet were soaring. She had to escape. *This must be it*, she presumed, stumbling through an open doorway. The sharp odor of chlorine hit her nostrils—that same smell that made her stomach churn as a child. Over thirty years had passed since then, but the strong memories still haunted her—even now as she raced blindly through the empty building.

Then she heard a thud. "Aaaiiieee!" she yelped, skidding to a stop. Next came a vibrating sound: *Doooiiing...doooiiing.* She thought it was her body, teetering after such a violent collision. She reached down to rub her toe. It had slammed into something hard. But the sound came from something lurking in front of her nose. She ran her fingers over the offending object she had just hit. Its contours were rigid and sharp.

When her eyes adjusted to the darkness, she could just make out its form. It was a metallic sign. She squinted to read the bold print.

"Rule number one: No running around the pool." *I'll remember that one*, she thought as the pain intensified in her toe.

Hélène scanned her surroundings. *Now, where am I going to hide?* Except for tiny rays of light filtering from its high windows, the pool area was completely dark. Spinning around, she spotted a large crate filled with swimming props just a few feet behind her. She ran behind it and crouched into a ball. Trying to ignore her racing heart, she squinted at the faint yellow light pouring down. At that instant, a strange thought popped into her head. *Now I know why I write poetry. So I can turn into an imaginary butterfly and exit my life through a grimy window.*

This thought preceded a deluge of additional early-morning reflections, each more far-fetched than the other. Finally, her imagination ran out of steam. *I'm too old for this,* she decided at last. Ignoring her throbbing toe, she stood. Just then, she heard a *whizz,* then a crackle, and a row of overhead lights popped on. Ducking down again, she noticed a hole in the bottom of the crate. She leaned her body sideways on the cold concrete floor. As she pressed her eye into the hole, she saw the fuzzy outline of a large pool. Then she gasped. *The yellow and green flip-flops.*

Craning her neck, Hélène's eyes shifted upward, following the tan ankles and muscular calves, leading up to… Hélène gulped at the figure sitting on a bench. *It's her.* She knew it even before she saw her face. Hélène pinched her ear to make sure she wasn't hallucinating. *Ouch.* Sure enough, this olive-skinned individual clad in a simple yellow swimsuit was the woman from the market, the jogger, the Greek stranger, with an incredibly athletic body. Hélène's palms began to sweat as her eyes scrutinized the mysterious woman.

Even though a swim cap hid that gorgeous dark hair, her striking body and exotic Greek nose made Hélène's body tremble. She had never had a reaction like this just from looking at someone. Not even Marc. Not even at the beginning, when they first met. A series of thoughts ran through her mind. *Why am I trembling like this? Because it's freezing in here? Because I'm lying on this cold concrete floor? Because my toe is throbbing? Or because I'm in shock because the Greek goddess is in here, right in front of me, with such…*

Hélène felt nauseous. Her hand went to her mouth.

Averting her eyes, she tried to shut out the faint *tap tap tap* as the tan toes in the flip-flops hit the floor with each passing second. She shivered. *Now what am I supposed to do?*

❖

Sylvie felt the cool air run over her thighs through the wooden slats in the bench. She wrapped her bath towel around her shoulders. A few minutes passed. She checked her watch. It was already 7:05 a.m. Shivering under her towel, she glanced at the women's locker room entrance. Still nobody. *She'd better show up*, she decided, already regretting her decision to take on this new student. But she needed the extra hours; she couldn't afford to refuse the job. Nursing images of herself snuggling under her cozy comforter with Goldie, she sighed. *I'd so much rather be in bed right now.* Hugging her elbows to her muscular chest, she tried to trap the warmth. *If she doesn't come by 7:15, I'm taking off. I could still go for a quick jog to the park.*

❖

From behind her crate filled with pool props, Hélène's eyes were glued on the Greek goddess. To her dismay, the toe tapping got worse, until finally, the goddess rose. Hélène's heart pounded as she watched the younger woman leave the pool area. Just as the goddess entered the women's locker room, Hélène emerged from behind the crate, cleared her throat, and hollered, *"Er...Excusez-moi."*

Sylvie reappeared, with a startled expression. *"Bonjour.* Where did you—" she began, glancing toward the men's locker room.

"Sorry I'm late," Hélène stammered. "I had difficulties finding the pool, *vous voyez*. Sort of took a detour. It was dark and—"

"Don't worry." With a warm smile, Sylvie held out her hand. "*Madame* Dupont? I'm Sylvie. I'll be teaching you to swim." Hélène drank in every bit of the goddess's sensuous voice.

Sylvie? Doesn't sound very Greek.

Before her knees could buckle, Hélène stepped backward. "*Bonjour.* I'm..." Fighting a froglike sensation in her throat, she squeaked, "I'm Hélène." As soon as Sylvie's strong fingers clasped hers, time stopped for Hélène—as if in a dream. She felt Sylvie's warm breath caressing her face, light and soft as a silken scarf floating in the breeze. She felt her lungs pumping fresh air under her swimming suit. Her legs were as weak as soggy cardboard. She leaned against the wall to keep from falling.

❖

"*Enchantée*, Hélène," chirped Sylvie, oblivious of the entrancing effect she had on her new student. She was too absorbed with the eyes behind Hélène's lenses. Their blueness startled her; she had never seen such an extraordinary deep-sea tint. The intensity created a potent cocktail of beauty mixed with fear. *It's normal. She's scared of the water*, she decided, pushing all other thoughts out of her mind. She smiled at her new protégée with the confidence of an expert instructor. *And that's why I'm here.*

❖

Hélène forced herself to return to reality. Awkwardly, she returned her teacher's smile. She was about to say, *"En fait, we've already met,"* but stopped. Feeling the goddess's eyes penetrating hers, she shifted her weight from one foot to the other.

"Nice pool."

Sylvie's early-morning voice was scratchy, with a slight Greek accent. "Brand new. *Alors,* you've never swum before?"

"Never. I've always hated water. It's embarrassing…I've always been scared of it."

Sylvie smiled. "You'll get used to it in no time." Sitting at the edge of the pool, she plopped her feet into the water. "Come have a seat." But Hélène remained at a distance, observing her teacher's tan feet as they kicked the surface. *"Venez,* have a seat," Sylvie repeated, gazing up at her student and tapping the space beside her. "I don't bite."

Ah, mon Dieu. Hélène glanced at Sylvie's muscular chest inside her tight bathing suit. *Here goes…* She made a silent wish, shut her eyes, and plopped herself next to the shapely tan thighs on the concrete. Lifting her toes into the air, she winced as she inched them toward the water.

CHAPTER EIGHT

The two scantily clad women were nearly pressed together. Hélène could feel Sylvie's body heat mixing with her own. From the corner of her eye, she could see Sylvie's neckline. Her yellow suit enhanced her dark skin, reminding Hélène of something she had recently written about a bumblebee: *Brown and yellow and fuzzy all over. Inviting, yet painful, when you finally feel the sting.*

Hélène also noticed how Sylvie's strong swimmer's chest extended the fabric in all the right places. She didn't dare look down at her own chest. She struggled to keep her eyes on the pool as the translucent water evoked childhood feelings of despair. *Deep, mesmerizing darkness.* Squeezing her eyes, she shuddered.

Sylvie whispered. "Just put your feet in. You'll feel better once you do."

"But I'm scared. I've always been afr—"

"I'm a lifeguard. If anything happens, I promise, I'll save you."

The tenderness in the instructor's voice gave Hélène courage. Ever so slowly, she lowered a toe into the water. "*Mince*, it's cold!" she yelped.

Sylvie chuckled. "You'll get used to it."

Toe by toe, Hélène gradually inserted her feet into the water.

"That wasn't so bad, *n'est-ce pas?*"

"Sure, if that's all I have to do every morning. Can I go home now?" blurted Hélène.

Sylvie tapped Hélène's knee. "I'm afraid there's more to it. *Mais ne vous inquiétez pas*, we'll go slowly. Every day we'll do a little more." With this, a jolt of electricity ran through Hélène's body. "And I promise you," continued Sylvie, gazing into Hélène's eyes, "you'll be swimming up a storm in no time. I'll be with you every step of the way."

She tapped Hélène's knee again. Hélène gulped. The electricity swept up her torso, straight to her cheeks. While her feet dangled in cold water, her face broke out in a sweat. She imagined the goddess with her in the water, grabbing her, locking her powerful arms around her chest. Instantly, she felt queasy.

"Hey, you don't look so good. *Ca va?*"

"I think my body's in shock," replied Hélène, trying to keep her mind off the water, Sylvie's soft brown eyes, and the intimate distance between their bodies. Sweat was trickling down her back. She wrapped her shoulders with her towel to fight off the chill.

"*Ne vous inquiétez pas.* Don't worry." Sylvie leaned closer. "Have we met somewhere before?"

Hélène's body froze. She could feel her neck hairs bristling under her tight swimming cap.

Sylvie lightly touched her shoulder. "*Je suis désolée.* It's only your first lesson and—

Hélène gave her a blank look. "*Excusez-moi*, what did you say?"

"I have the feeling we've already met."

"*Enfin,* actually…" Hélène started blushing.

"Did we?"

Hélène gripped the side of the pool. "A few weeks ago, at the market. We met at the flower stand and—"

"You found my keychain!" blurted Sylvie, slapping her thigh. "I didn't recognize you with your swim cap on."

Hélène tried to suppress her nervousness. "Me neither. We were both wearing clothes."

"*Quelle coïncidence!*" Sylvie smiled, revealing a cute pair of dimples. "You saved my life that day."

"I wouldn't go that far. Besides…" Hélène gestured at the pool. "You'll be saving mine from now on."

"Let's hope not. But I'll always be here if you need me." Sylvie stretched her chest muscles. "*Allez-y,* let's give it a try."

❖

Sylvie entered the shallow water and held out her arms. Hélène took a deep breath and grabbed her teacher's hands. "It's freezing!" she cried as the water hit her knees.

"It's not that bad."

Hélène shook her head. "It's like bathing in an iced tea."

Sylvie let go of her student's hands. "How poetic! Are you a writer?"

She's got to be kidding. "I just scribble."

"As in books?"

"Poems. Just silly stuff, really."

Sylvie's dimples materialized. "I love poetry."

Hélène's eyes perked up. "Really?"

"That's so cool." Sylvie's eyes lingered on Hélène's. "But let's get back to our swimming lesson. *Suivez-moi.*" She walked backward.

Hélène took a deep breath, trying to control her awkward moves in the water. She lifted her arms for balance. *I give up,* she decided, stalling.

"*Allez-y.* You can do it," seizing her hands, Sylvie ventured deeper—up to her waist.

Grimacing, Hélène inched forward, one toe at a time.

Sylvie took a bigger step; Hélène started to topple.

"Got ya!" Sylvie caught her.

Feeling the Greek goddess's strong arms around her chest, Hélène's mind flashed back to the market a few weeks before. *Forbidden...*

A sea of foreign sensations swept through her body, invading it like a tidal wave washing over a city, sweeping away all that wasn't firmly fastened down. Hélène struggled to keep her feet on the ground. She was transported to another time zone in Sylvie's arms.

Then she felt a burst of warm air on her lips.

But instead of exotic spices from a faraway land, all Hélène could detect was chlorine. After what seemed like hours, they pulled their wet bodies apart and gazed at each other. *I can't believe this is happening.*

Sylvie broke the silence. "*Ca va?*"

"Sorry. I'm such a wimp." Hélène shifted her hips.

"Not at all. Remember, this is new to you. And you're doing great. *Suivez-moi.*"

Sylvie walked backward again. Whenever Hélène faltered, Sylvie grabbed her. Soon, they were soaked to the ears. In between laughs, Hélène ventured, "Can I ask you a question?"

"*Bien sûr.*"

"It's kind of personal."

This made Sylvie stop laughing. Abruptly, her eyes lost their youthful sparkle and turned serious.

❖

Ah, non. Not again, thought Sylvie. She cupped her hands and squirted a thin stream of water across the pool. How she always hated this. Things would be going great until her new students—usually those taking private lessons—would ask her a series of inevitable questions about her personal life: *Married? Children?—C'est bizarre. Why not?*

She squared her shoulders, bracing herself for the onslaught of invasive queries. It always happened on the second or third lesson. *She seemed different from the others. Yet she's asking me this on our first day. Guess they're all the same. How in the heck does my private life have anything to do with swimming lessons?*

Sylvie realized how sensitive she was about this, but she couldn't help it. Raised in a huge Greek family with traditional values, she wasn't like her siblings. All her life, she had felt like a rarity—a hard raisin trapped in a loaf of fresh bread, an indigestible item to chew.

The question she hated most was: "When will you finally settle down with a nice man and start a family?" Yaya was the only person in Santorini who left her alone. She cooked up healthy dishes of advice, like most grandmas, but she never forced intimate details out of Sylvie. Rather than imposing her ideas, she would scatter precious seeds of counsel—as if nourishing a baby bird. Sylvie was free to nibble or not.

Even though Sylvie resided in Brussels, thousands of kilometers away, she always sensed the vibrations of Yaya's unfaltering love and respect. Unfortunately, the rest of Sylvie's family—and even her neighbors—thought it was their right as Greeks to know everything. Her throat tightened just thinking about it. Fifteen years ago, she had naïvely thought she would escape this nonsense when she moved to Belgium. But here it was, happening again.

"I don't want to be rude or anything but..."

Sylvie squinted. *Merde. Here it comes.*

"You have a bit of an accent. Are you from somewh—"

"*Oui!*" Sylvie burst out. "I'm from Greece. And I'm actually a big, wild, Greek dolphin."

Before Hélène could respond, Sylvie dove underwater and swam around Hélène's legs. After a while, she resurfaced. Pulling off her cap, she shook her hair, releasing a luscious cascade of dark silk. Gasping for air, she turned to face Hélène, who stood mesmerized by the droplets running down her muscular chest.

❖

Hélène's body reacted like she had just downed a bottle of whiskey. She couldn't tear her eyes from the pair of erect nipples aiming straight at her. Even through her water-smeared lenses, she detected the buds poking through the thin yellow fabric. Her head started whizzing as she fell backward.

Sylvie grabbed her and whispered in her ear. "*Ca va?* I didn't mean to scare you."

Hélène tried to focus. "Just feeling kind of dizzy."

"Did you have breakfast this morning?"

Hélène remembered feeding Chaussette. *But did I eat?* "Guess I didn't."

"Tomorrow I want you to eat breakfast first. Cereal or fruit—bananas are good."

Hélène nodded.

"That's enough for today." Sylvie guided her to the shallow end. "You did great. See you tomorrow."

Hélène climbed out of the pool. *Hope she doesn't notice my big butt.* She quickly covered up with her towel. When she turned around, Sylvie was nowhere in sight.

There she is. She held her breath as a flash of yellow soared through the water. Powerful arms carved the surface, each stroke leaving a frothy mark.

Hélène shivered on the cold concrete. *So graceful and strong.* As she tiptoed toward the locker room, painfully aware of her sore toe, she sidestepped the warning sign: "Rule number one: No running around the pool."

CHAPTER NINE

Bundled like a baby in a fluffy bathrobe, Cecile stood amidst half a dozen fake palm trees. Puddles of water enveloped her dainty feet after a late-night plunge in her private outdoor pool. She shook her brown curls like a poodle, flicking chlorinated droplets at the plastic trees. A blissful cry erupted from her throat until ringing interrupted her folly.

She sashayed over to a gold-rimmed, retro telephone.

"Cecile Beaucils," she answered, rousing her most feminine voice. "I'm so glad you called!" Her tone dropped half an octave. "*Attends.* Slow down, *ma puce.*"

Cecile squinted at the moon. "So how was your first lesson?" she asked, twisting her hair into a tight ringlet. "*Quoi?* You're kidding. The woman at the market?"

Smacking her delicate lips together, she eased into a lounge chair. "Go ahead. I'm all ears."

❖

Marc's mustache rose and fell in tiny, rapid movements— like a rabbit's nose. Hélène concentrated on his thin lips, which seemed to be scowling. *Wonder if it's because of what he's reading or what he's chewing?* She reached for her fork.

Tonight, she would do things differently: she would focus on her food instead of *him*.

What a reward. Her taste buds serenaded each carefully prepared morsel. The tender steak, fresh zucchini, and whole-wheat pasta that miraculously turned out *al dente*. Licking her soft lips, she took it all in. Now that she was biking to work—after purging her junk food stashes—her appetite skyrocketed. She was inhaling healthy snacks: handfuls of mixed nuts, dried fruit, a banana, or half an avocado with whole-wheat wafers. Just as Dr. Duprès predicted, with exercise and a healthier diet, Hélène's energy level soared.

As she shoveled pasta into her mouth, her thoughts went back to the morning's swimming lesson for the umpteenth time. All she had to do was close her eyes, and the Greek goddess materialized, hands outstretched and zealous, to transport her into the water.

Hélène's reverie was interrupted by a grunt. "Where's the sauce?" Marc was waving a forkful of steak at her.

"*Comment?*" muttered Hélène, lifting her eyelids. "*Désolée, chéri.* Did you say something?"

"You know I can't eat my meat without Béarnaise."

"*Chéri*, remember what the doctor said? I need to be careful, so I'm trying to—"

"Poison me with these new recipes of yours? Couldn't get any blander." Marc mashed the zucchini on his plate.

"You've just got to get used to the natural taste of real food. It's wholesome, with no additives or excess calories. I've been reading a lot about it, actually. Japanese cuisine is—"

"Who cares about Japanese cuisine? We're in Belgium, remember? So I want Belgian food. Like *frites*, mayonnaise, Béarnaise sauce, *chicons au gratin...*"

"*S'il te plaît, chéri.* Try to understand. Dr. Duprès insisted on this. And if my blood test results are better, we can go back to eating sauces again."

"You had *better* get good results. This stuff reeks." Marc threw his napkin down.

As soon as he was gone, Hélène glanced at his plate. He had hardly touched it, except to mash the pasta and zucchini together, sculpting the mass into a three-dimensional form. She looked at the odd shape and shrugged. *Guess he really is an artist.*

"By the way," added Marc, returning from the kitchen with bulging cheeks and armfuls of potato chips, ice cream, and several beers. "I forgot to congratulate you." As he munched, he waved his ice-cream scooper at Hélène. "I see you didn't drown this morning."

With a spring in his step, he disappeared into the living room.

❖

Sylvie sat on the cold bench, dangling her feet. She pulled her towel around her thighs to keep warm.

At precisely 7:02, Hélène tiptoed out of the locker room. Sylvie jumped up and kissed her on the cheek. "Glad you're back!"

Mon Dieu! Hélène wasn't expecting a kiss. When she stood stiff as a statue, Sylvie backtracked. "Sorry, that must have sounded strange. It's just that after their first lesson, some students decide that swimming's not for them. Especially older..."

Hélène's face fell.

"*Désolée*, I didn't mean that."

"That's okay." Averting Sylvie's eyes, Hélène looked at

her toes. They seemed so pale on the concrete, almost bluish. *I could probably be her mother.*

"That's not what I meant," repeated Sylvie. "I'm thirty-six myself."

Hélène looked up. "I'm forty." Saying it made her feel even older. *At least I couldn't be her mother.*

"Ah, you're so ancient." Sylvie flashed her a smile, exposing her dimples. But the smile quickly faded. "Just kidding! You don't look anywhere near forty," she insisted, apparently trying to erase the damage. "You don't look even look thirty."

"Has anyone ever informed you that you're a rotten liar?"

"What counts is how we *feel*." Sylvie inhaled deeply and stretched her arms. "I promise, once you start swimming, you'll feel fantastic. You'll grow younger by the day."

Hélène shivered, not knowing if it was due to the chilly morning air on her bare skin or the fact that the goddess kept inching closer to her.

"So let's get started. Go take a seat on the bench."

Standing before her, Sylvie casually removed her towel.

Hélène caught her breath. Her instructor's olive-skinned body looked even more magnificent today, as if a sculptor had spent years crafting it, chiseling it in all the right places. Such strong shoulders; such a slim waist. *She sure is a swimmer.* Her powerful thighs were inches from Hélène's nose. Remembering her own flabby legs, she wished she could shrink to the size of a pea.

"Ahem." Sylvie stood with her arms folded. "*Aujourd'hui*, I'm going to show you how to breathe underwater." Her voice deepened. "It's easy. You just breathe in over your shoulder, and breathe out under the water—like this." Leaning forward, she extended her bicep, twisted her head, and inhaled deeply. Then she turned toward the ground and exhaled.

"Keep your chin in and only breathe through your mouth."
After repeating this three times, it was Hélène's turn.

Hélène stiffened when she felt Sylvie's breath on her neck. No matter how hard she tried, her chest refused to expel the air trapped in her lungs.

"Exhale harder. I can't hear you," instructed Sylvie, placing a warm hand on Hélène's back. This only made things worse. Immobilized, Hélène stopped breathing.

"Let's try that again," said Sylvie.

Hélène did the exercise perfectly.

"*Bien.* Now it's time to try it out for real," said Sylvie, leading Hélène down the steps.

Tiny bubbles floated to the surface as she exhaled in the shallow water.

When her teacher stood at last, Hélène couldn't help but stare at the droplets pouring down Sylvie's magnificent body. As if in a trance, her poetic mind wandered to deep, uncharted depths...

❖

Sylvie pondered Hélène's droopy eyelids. *She didn't hear a word I said. If those are "bedroom eyes," I can't even imagine what that guy does to her to put her in this state.* Sylvie shuddered at the thought.

When Hélène donned an old-fashioned, black rubber diving mask, Sylvie bit her lip to keep from giggling. *She's a real kick.*

But as soon as her student's nose hit the water, she ripped off the mask. "I can't do this!"

"Yes, you can. Try again." Sylvie placed her hand on her shoulder. *Poor thing. She's quivering. I've got to check the pool temperature.*

"Tell me when I'm supposed to start enjoying this," grumbled Hélène. Reluctantly, she donned her mask again and slid her face into the water. As instructed, she turned her head and inhaled. But instead of air, she got a lungful of chlorinated water. As water gushed from her mouth, she sputtered, "*Vous voyez!* I knew I couldn't do it!"

"The first time's the hardest, I promise. *Allez-y*, let's try again."

Hélène came up choking again. "I'll never get this!" She threw her mask at the deep end of the pool, where it began to sink. Then she burst into tears.

Sylvie placed her arm around her pupil's shoulders. "*Ne vous inquiétez pas*. It'll be okay," she said in a soothing tone. "You'll get it. It's really not that hard."

"That's easy for you to say."

"Watch me," said Sylvie, diving into the shallow water. In just a few strokes, she retrieved the mask at the bottom of the pool. Gently, she placed Hélène's diving mask back on her face. "*Voilà.* You're all set."

"This is the last time." Hélène grimaced. "If it doesn't work, I'm giving up."

"Deal."

"I'd probably be better at Rollerblading anyway."

"I'm sure you would. All aspiring poets are," replied Sylvie, chuckling. "Now stick your head in the water before I do it for you!"

Hélène took a quick breath and lowered her head. This time, she did the exercise as instructed. Triumphantly, she began jumping and threw her arms around Sylvie's neck. "I did it!"

What enthusiasm, mused Sylvie. *Just like a kid.* Then Sylvie noticed a tingling sensation: her pupil's breasts were rubbing against hers as she jumped in the water. With Hélène's arms still around her neck, the friction between their bodies stimulated her in tender spots that she knew shouldn't be stimulated during private swimming lessons. Especially with straight students—married or not.

Delicately, Sylvie pushed her away. "That's super, Hélène. But I think we've had enough excitement for today, *n'est-ce pas?*" Before her pupil could respond, Sylvie dove back in the water to cool off.

❖

Lydia sat pouting in her new gold BMW as she scanned the trees through her steamy windshield. "She should be here by now," she muttered under her breath. Impulsively, she raised her newly manicured nails to her lips. But before their tips entered her mouth, she noticed the silky pink polish. "Darn, I gave that up."

She hugged herself to keep warm in her new gold Chanel jogging outfit. "I didn't get up at dawn and drive all this way for my health."

At last, she spotted a woman with a ponytail running on the other side of the park.

"*Enfin!*" she exclaimed, jumping out of her car and jogging across the grass. Then she stopped abruptly and bent down. "This is pure torture. How can anyone enjoy this?" She pulled on her socks to keep her new jogging shoes from chewing up her ankles.

"*Mince*, it's not her," muttered Lydia as the woman jogged passed her. "But she's kind of cute..." she muttered, trudging after her.

After a few seconds, Chanel woman got a cramp and had to give up the chase. She plopped herself on a bench and whipped out her golden cell phone. She pursed her lips as her slender pink fingernails made the familiar clicking noises on the keys. "I'm such a femme fatale."

With each empty ring, however, Lydia's lips tightened. She struggled to force the anger from her mind. As usual, it was a fierce battle. Her temples were throbbing with rage.

At the end of Sylvie's recorded message, Lydia cleared her throat and flashed her fakest smile at the nearest victim—a tree. "*Salut, mon lapin*, where *are* you?" she gushed into the receiver. "I'm here at the park—*our* park—waiting for you. Please call me back, honey bunny, *d'accord*? It's been days and I'm worried about you, my little pump—"

Just then, the jogger in a ponytail ran past Lydia. Without hesitating, Lydia jumped up. "Kin," she added under her breath as she and her Chanel suit promptly chased after the ponytail.

❖

Hélène was styling her hair with a blow-dryer when something moved behind her. She reached for her glasses and saw Sylvie's glistening face in the mirror.

Hélène gulped. The only thing separating her from the goddess's nakedness was a white towel—and two inches of steam. Sylvie's wet, silky hair spilled off her firm shoulders. She gave her dark locks a shake.

"You did great today."

"What?" Hélène switched off the blow-dryer. She tried to keep her eyes off her teacher—without success. She could feel her pupils dilating as if to swallow Sylvie in their depths.

"I'm embarrassed." Hélène blushed. "I acted just like a baby."

"Not at all," Sylvie put her hand on Hélène's shoulder. "It's not easy at first. Not for anyone. You did great. *Vraiment.*"

The warm hand radiated through Hélène's blouse,

penetrating her skin. She quivered. Then Sylvie gave her a little wink and tiptoed toward the bathroom stalls.

Before Hélène had a chance to recover, she heard buzzing. She glanced toward the stalls. *That's a weird tinkle.* Then she shook her head. *Mais non.* She put the blow-dryer next to her ear. *It's not this.* The buzzing continued. She spotted Sylvie's yellow backpack on the counter. *Sounds like a cell phone.* She reached toward the zipper.

Wonder who's calling her?

Hélène's fingers hovered over the pocket.

❖

What am I thinking? Hélène quickly withdrew her hand. As a consolation, she picked up the keychain lying next to the backpack. The metal fish's smoothness felt somehow reassuring. As her fingers caressed its lustrous surface, a surge of vitality swept through her body, drawing her mind like a magnet back to the moment when the two women first met.

Hélène shut her eyes to capture the images flashing by, like a storyboard for a film.

A flicker of light from the exotic woman's eyes—rich as dark chocolate—reaches out to grab her. Hélène's body is transported to the lands of ancient Greece. Her throat goes dry. A soft, sandy wind blows around her body; when she tenses, something inside her cracks. She's immobile on the outside, vulnerable from within. The goddess's eyes mesmerize her. With her sensuous, wet lips...

Abruptly, Hélène caught her breath. Sylvie was standing right behind her, grinning. Her dark skin contrasted beautifully with the white towel barely concealing her muscular contours.

And her luscious hair, now whipped up in a white towel, created the spitting image of a movie star.

With horror, Hélène realized her cheek was twitching again. But she completely forgot her tic when she noticed what was in her palm. *Mon Dieu!*

She flung the keychain on the counter as if it were a dead tarantula.

Sylvie chuckled. "Remember that day?" She waved her comb at the silver keychain. "Isn't life bizarre? Who would've thought—"

"I know. Such a coincidence." *Please, don't let her see my tic*, thought Hélène as Sylvie plopped down next to her, unraveling her head towel.

"Now it's my turn to ask you a question." Sylvie turned to face Hélène, who swiveled sideways to hide her pulsating cheek. "Who was that guy at the café?"

"Guy? What guy?"

"At the market, with the skinny mustache—"

"Ah...Marc," muttered Hélène to the wall.

"Marc?"

"*Oui*, Marc," replied Hélène. As she repeated his name, she felt something give way in her cheek, followed by a bland sensation. *Bizarre. Tic's gone. All I had to say was his name.*

Hélène felt her teacher's eyes on hers. *Better get it over with.* "He's my husband."

Sylvie's brows were knitted together. "I figured."

"*Ah, bon?* Is it that obvious?"

Sylvie opened her mouth to reply, but Hélène beat her to it. "Brussels sure is small," she declared, changing the subject. "It's like a village, don't you think? Hard to imagine it's actually the capital of Europe."

Sylvie nodded. "Never know who you'll run into. How often do you go to the market?"

"Every Saturday. What about you?" Hélène's voice cracked. She became even more vigilant of her thoughts, lest they spread to her facial muscles again.

"*Moi aussi.* Every Saturday."

"*C'est bizarre.* Wonder why we've never run into each other before."

"Who knows? Maybe we did but didn't realize it." Sylvie's cheeks widened, exposing her dimples. "When I get to the flower stand, all I see are luscious plants everywhere. It's like I become one with them. I'm blinded by their beauty, and—"

"Me too, it's like somehow, they enter a deeper part of my being, and I lose all notion of time," Hélène added with an exuberant squeal. "It drives my husband insane."

Sylvie's eyebrows narrowed. "So we've probably seen each other before but didn't realize it."

C'est impossible, thought Hélène, trying to keep her eyes off the Greek goddess's bare shoulders. *I would have remembered you. That's for sure.*

Sylvie dangled her keys. "I'm glad we did. I'd have never seen these again!" She kissed the silvery fish.

Seeing this, Hélène got a queasy feeling in her stomach. She jumped up. "Time to go. I'm going to be late—" The locker room door slammed. "For work!"

Sylvie sat on her stool, brows knitted, facing herself in the mirror. After a brief hesitation, she grabbed her bathrobe and ran after her.

❖

Dark orange flickers of light danced into Hélène's eyes, reflecting the sun's early-morning efforts to illuminate the city. Standing under a tree, Hélène shielded her eyes from the soft ball rising in the sky. She wished she could snatch its comforting warmth, to keep her from feeling things she shouldn't be feeling. *I wish Maman were here.*

The crunch of gravel made her jump.

"Thought you were in a hurry."

Hélène swung around to face Sylvie, in her bathrobe. She stammered, "Well, I—"

"Glad you're still here. You forgot this."

"I'm so absentminded." Hélène took her bag. "*Merci,*" she muttered, avoiding her teacher's inquisitive eyes. When she bent down to unlock her bike, she heard a throat clear.

"Your husband doesn't like plants, *n'est-ce pas?*"

Where did that come from? Hélène stiffened. "He says they're a waste of money."

"I couldn't live without mine." Sylvie reached and tweaked a leaf-covered branch. A yellow leaf swirled down, landing in her pupil's hair. "They're my best buddies."

"Me too. Especially flowers." Hélène stood. The leaf fell off her head.

Sylvie chuckled. "If I had to choose between flowers and meals, I'd rather starve."

"Looks like you've already made your choice," said Hélène, pointing to Sylvie's slim waist, despite her bulky bathrobe. "And I've made mine. Just look at this fat belly!"

Sylvie gripped Hélène's handlebars. "Once you start swimming every day, you'll lose it."

"But I've never had a flat stomach. Not even as a kid." Hélène pinched a fold in her stomach. "Just rolling rubber."

"You never swam before. You'll lose it, I promise."

"Sure hope so." Hélène swung a leg over her bike, expecting Sylvie to move, but she didn't. "*Attention,* you'll get bike grease on you."

Sylvie chuckled, exposing her dimples. "Do I seem like

the kind of gal who's afraid to get her clothes dirty?" She leaned over the handlebars, exposing a glimpse of bosom surrounded by soft, white terry cloth. Her legs were straddling the bike's front wheel.

Hélène's heart started racing. Muted, she shook her head. A droplet slid out of her ear.

I must be waterlogged.

Finally, she broke the awkward silence. Wiggling her handlebars, she declared unconvincingly, "I'd better get to work."

Sylvie peered into her eyes. "You know, Hélène, if you work hard enough, you can do anything you want."

"What do you mean?"

"You just need a bit more confidence."

"Aren't you supposed to be a swimming instructor?" Hélène started blushing. "Don't tell me you teach philosophy too?"

"*Non*, I just say what I think. And I think—"

"I really do have to go," Hélène snapped. To her relief, the olive-skinned hands released her handlebars. Hélène dug her feet into the pedals, and the bike raced forward.

"Didn't mean to offend you," declared Sylvie.

"Just forget about it, *d'accord*?" Gravel flew as Hélène rode off.

"Who does she think she is?" Hélène muttered as she pedaled down the street. *I've got everything I need in my—*

Before she could finish her thought, a sharp *craaaack* erupted overhead and a streak of lightning sliced through the sky. A raindrop splattered Hélène's glasses.

The drops soon became buckets. *Soggy Belgian summers.* Hélène pedaled even more furiously. Racing through mud puddles, she left all traces of Sylvie behind—or so she thought.

❖

When Hélène finally reached her office, she sloshed her way into the ladies' room, ignoring the puddles her boots left on the linoleum. She faced the mirror defiantly. *Time for the tornado effect.* Laughing frantically at her glistening face, she shook her body like a wild dog, flinging her hair in all directions. Water droplets splatted the mirrors.

Voilà. I feel much lighter now. She disappeared into a stall.

Hélène reappeared in a skirt and promptly applied glossy peach lipstick. Parting her wet, shiny lips, she whispered "olive juice" into the mirror, three times. Each time, she accentuated the "o" and the "ju" even more slowly and sexily, opening and closing her soft, round lips. *Just like Marilyn Monroe,* she mused, blowing exaggerated kisses at herself.

"*Embrassez-moi, chérie.* Just one kiss and I'll be your slave forever!" Hélène whispered in a raspy voice. She puckered her peachy lips and gave the mirror a full-on kiss.

Sounds of spiky heels on linoleum approached. Hélène ripped her lips from the moist glass. Cecile stood directly behind her. After a quick look at Hélène—and her evidence of passion on the mirror—she shrieked and did an about-face.

"Ahhh!" she screamed as her spikes slid on the slippery floor. Her alarmed face headed toward the linoleum.

"Gotcha!" Hélène lunged, grabbing her colleague's tiny waist.

The two women stood clinging to each other and panting. After a few awkward seconds, Cecile pulled away. "*Merci,*" she mumbled, cringing.

"Nice artwork." She pointed to the oval peach smudge on the mirror. Then she flashed a confused smile at Hélène before tiptoeing into a stall.

❖

Sure is hot in here. Sylvie opened the neckline of her bathrobe. Her wet hair tumbled down, cooling her skin. She turned the yellowed pages ever so thoughtfully. As she took in each enticing poem, she became oblivious to all around her. Every few lines, she closed her eyes to better consume the author's delicate prose. The howling wind outside, flinging sheets of raindrops against the locker room's windows, intensified the poem's enchanting effects.

It was only when she heard a bird's faint cry that she looked up.

Then something smashed into the locker room window. Sylvie ran outside.

Right below the window, a small form lay on the muddy soil. It was a baby chick. Sylvie swooped it up, amazed at how light it felt in her fingers—like a piece of fluff. She inspected the lemony ball of fuzz. Its miniature red beak opened and shut.

It's trying to say something. But no sound came out, not even a peep.

Sylvie's heart melted. *"Salut, ma petite,"* she whispered, gently stroking its head.

Rain pounded on Sylvie's head. Drops trickled down her face. Hunching over, she sheltered the chick in her arms. As water slid down her bathrobe, a chill ran through her.

But Sylvie didn't care. She was focused on the tiny creature in her hands, the chick's warm chest against her own. Its heart was beating rapidly, like an overwound watch.

She's like Yaya—soft and gentle, weak and fragile. Despite the sloshing noises filling her ears, Sylvie thought she heard a voice. She lifted her head but saw nobody in the downpour.

Then, ever so faintly, she recognized the words of Yaya, her grandmother: "Soak up the pleasurable moments in life, honey. Every little bit. Make 'em seep through your pores till you burst." Sylvie looked at the furious rain clouds. Water streamed into her eyes, smarting them.

"All right, Yaya, you got my attention. I'm soaking 'em up."

The elderly woman's voice continued, "Especially, don't be afraid of love. You never know when it'll come, so when it hits you, make sure you grab it, honey. With both hands."

I'm grabbing, Yaya. I'm grabbing. Sylvie cradled the frail creature solemnly.

The voice concluded, "'Cause you never know when it's leaving you for good."

Sylvie placed her ear on the chick's tiny wet chest. The heartbeat was gone.

As its body began to chill in her hands, Sylvie felt pain erupt in her own chest. She choked back a sob. Desperate to bring the bird's precious life back to Earth, she pushed her fingertips deep into the chick's flesh as she stroked its feathers. But her efforts proved futile.

Standing in the mud, she gave in to her emotions— something she hadn't done in years. *I feel so empty.* She pressed her face next the chick's body one last time. *Come back*, she pleaded, but its tiny life was over.

After a pensive moment, Sylvie realized she was shivering. Her eyelids were so cold, they refused to cry anymore. She found a drier spot on the ground and, ever so gently, set the chick down. After covering its body with damp leaves, she took one last look at its burial place and went inside to thaw out.

❖

"*Bonjour.*" Hélène rescued an orange flower that had gravitated to the carpet. "Bet you're as bored as me, *n'est-ce pas?* Let's take a walk." Humming, she sauntered off toward the office kitchen. She plopped the flower in a glass of water, then went to the coffee machine.

Abruptly, she stopped humming. *Ah oui, I'm supposed to stay away from this.*

Reluctantly, she poured the smooth black liquid into the sink. Squeezing her eyes shut, she inhaled its tangy aroma. *Roasted beans, roasted bliss.* When she lifted her lids, a trail of darkness was winding down the drain. *Mince, what a waste.* She rummaged in a cupboard until she unearthed a stray chamomile teabag. Unceremoniously, she dunked it in her mug.

Back at her desk, Hélène took a sip of herbal tea and scrunched her nose. *C'est affreux.*

"Maybe with a bit of sugar…" She fished around in her drawers. Ripping open a packet, she trickled the white powder into her cup. "*Voilà.* That's better," she exclaimed, four packets later.

After an hour of nonstop translating, Hélène pulled on her hair. *This is so dry, I could scream. Who cares anyway?* She clicked on her mouse. Her latest poem appeared on the screen: *The butterfly's sick of its current life. It's bored. It needs a huge change. More action. A bit of passion…*

She smiled at the flower she had rescued. *Much more exciting, non?*

❖

Sylvie scrutinized her face in the mirror. Grief made her full lips seem heavier. In their wetness, her eyebrows seemed bushier than usual. A swollen tear rode over her cheek, splattering onto the counter. Instantly, her mind reeled back, playing scenes of the past, unfurling the mighty sights, sounds, and smells of crashing waves, seagulls...

Greece, she thought. *Home*... Instead of cheering her up, a wave of nausea hit. As soon as she thought of the tiny, lifeless chick lying under damp leaves, panic hit.

Yaya! Just as she grabbed her cell phone, it buzzed in her hand.

One new message, it read. *Non. Please don't let this happen.* Sylvie took a deep breath, pushed Enter and then Loudspeaker.

"*Bonjour. Vous avez un nouveau message,*" announced the computerized voice. Sylvie held her breath as she waited for her message.

"*Salut, mon lapin*, where *are* you?"

Sylvie relaxed as soon as she recognized Lydia. *Never thought I'd be glad to hear that obnoxious voice again.*

"I'm here at the park—*our* park—waiting for you. *Téléphone-moi*, honey bunny, *d'accord*? It's been days, and I'm worried about—"

Behind Sylvie, someone cleared her throat.

The swimming instructor hit Off, chopping Lydia's voice mid-sentence. When Sylvie jumped up, her hair did a lasso whip, flinging rain around the locker room.

"*Pardon!*" she gasped at the woman standing before her.

"*Voyons, ma petite*, it can't be that bad." The older woman laced her arms around Sylvie, whose eyes were swollen from crying. Wiping the droplets off Sylvie's face, she smacked her cheek with a motherly kiss.

"I swear, in all these years, I've never seen you so melodramatic." Shaking her head, she sighed. "She's not worth it, I tell you."

Sylvie opened her mouth. "But—"

"*Shhh, ma petite.* Inge knows best," continued the heavy-set woman with a tight, gray bun, placing her finger over Sylvie's lips. "Besides, the herd's already in the water."

In her soft white bathrobe, Sylvie looked more like a Hollywood actress lamenting before her final scene than a certified swim coach. The only hint of her true profession was her footwear: yellow and green flip-flops. As soon as she heard "the herd," her eyes sparkled.

Inge, the older woman, squeezed her waist. "They're so excited about the new pool. We can't keep them waiting, *n'est-ce pas?*" She nudged Sylvie out of the locker room.

The clamor of fifty ten-year-olds roughhousing at the pool's edge shook Sylvie out of her misery. Her agile body braced itself for action.

"Come on, *les enfants. Calmez-vous!*" hollered Inge. "Is that how I taught you to greet your teacher? Now, what do we say?"

"*Bonjour, Mademoiselle Routard!*" yelled the group in unison.

Smiling at the sea of young faces before her, Sylvie forgot all about her poems, the tiny bird, and Yaya—for a few chaotic, yet exhilarating hours in the pool.

CHAPTER TEN

The next morning, a young couple on a tandem bicycle passed Hélène on the road.

Hélène stared at the girl hugging her boyfriend, ponytail swishing as the couple maneuvered through the dark. Hélène winced at the early-morning giggles blended with the slippery sounds of tires over damp pavement.

What happened to us? she wondered, remembering her recent fight with Marc. He had pounded his fist on the table; she had rescued the vase before it crashed, hugging the daisies to her chest until he stormed out. She winced again, feeling fresh pain as the two joyous cyclists—piled with camping gear—pedaled away.

❖

Sylvie was already in the water. *"Bonjour,"* she called as Hélène slowly entered the pool's cool water. She gave her a kiss on the cheek and handed her a yellow Styrofoam board. "Today we're learning how to kick." Clasping the side, she demonstrated the breaststroke with her legs.

"Wait." Hélène frowned. "That's not the stroke you were doing the other day."

"What do you mean?" When Sylvie stood, droplets ran down the front of her suit.

Hélène couldn't help noticing her teacher's chest muscles, so near and glistening wet. *Is she even real? Her body belongs in some sort of museum.* Realizing the goddess was still staring at her, Hélène stammered, "I…I was watching you. You were doing a different stroke." She took a step back.

"So you were spying on me, *eh*? How naughty!" Sylvie splashed a few drops at Hélène.

"*Non*, not at all!" Hélène laughed nervously. "When I was leaving, I saw you swimming. Like this." She imitated her teacher doing the freestyle.

"That's *le crawl*. I figured you'd want to learn the breaststroke first."

Breaststroke? Hélène glanced at her teacher's chest again—so smooth, so tan. She felt a hard knot in her stomach. "*Non*. I want to learn the crawl, like you."

"Okay, we'll do the crawl for now," Sylvie said, caressing her moist neck. "I'm sure we'll have plenty of time later to practice the breaststroke," she added with a wink.

Hélène felt a rush of adrenaline through her body.

Clasping the edge of the pool, Sylvie demonstrated how to do the scissor kick. Hélène imitated her. Laughing, they kicked until bubbles spewed everywhere. But when Sylvie showed her how to kick using a Styrofoam board, instead of moving forward, Hélène's body began to sink. She rose, gasping for air.

"Can you breathe?" Sylvie tapped her lightly on the back.

Water sputtered from Hélène's mouth. She nodded.

"*Bien*. Let's try again. I'll hold you this time." Sylvie opened her arms.

"*Non!*" Hélène exclaimed. "I mean…That's okay. I'm fine."

"Just till you get the hang of it." The goddess wrapped her arms around her waist. Hélène stiffened.

"*Allez,* just relax," whispered Sylvie. Hélène's body stiffened even more. "*Voilà.* I've got you. Breathe deeply and let the water support you."

Hélène let Sylvie bring her into the prone position. Clasping the board, she kicked, advancing slowly in the water.

"*C'est parfait,*" said Sylvie with satisfaction. "Now, try it on your own." She released her hands from Hélène's waist. Her student's body began to sink.

"Keep kicking!" ordered Sylvie.

Like a sputtering motor, Hélène's legs revved up. A rush of bubbles erupted near her feet. *I'm actually swimming!* The blond woman was beaming as she inched across the pool.

❖

Hélène was still on a high as she pedaled to work. The traffic signals kept turning red, but she didn't care. She had kicked across the pool four times—all by herself. She smiled at the thought of Sylvie, who had been so gentle and encouraging.

The streets were still dark, but a faint orange hue was just lifting to tint the sky.

At yet another red light, Hélène set her foot down. Startled, something hard was beneath it. She glanced down. Under her boot was a small picture frame. As she dusted off the glass, a painting gradually emerged.

Dozens of white houses were perched on a cliff, overlooking a vast blue sea.

Hélène ran her fingers over the rough waves, admiring their crashing white tips. It was painted in oil, with *Santorini 1983* written at the bottom.

She had always loved the seaside, though she rarely went. As a typical *Bruxelloise*, the hour and a half drive seemed too far for just a day, and Marc would never agree to staying at a hotel.

Her thoughts were interrupted by a honk. Only then did she notice the steady flow of cars racing past. She hastily looked around. Seeing no potential owners—just an overflowing trash can—she stuffed the frame into her jacket. *Guess you're mine*, she mused, cradling the painting to her chest like a newborn.

❖

Hélène unzipped her jacket and set her newfound treasure on her office desk directly in front of Marc's picture, which was tiny and bland compared to the gold-framed massive one adorning Chaussette, her black-and-white cat.

As Hélène waited for her computer to boot up, she imagined herself swimming through powerful waves, mastering the scissor kick alongside Sylvie, off the coast of an exotic island. A tingle of excitement ran down her spine. When the search engine finally appeared, her fingers couldn't type the word "Santorini" fast enough.

That evening, trees whipped past as she biked through Parc Cinquantenaire. Halfway through, she spotted a group practicing karate. "*Hi-yah!*" they yelled in unison, kicking their feet over their heads. One of the women in the back caught Hélène's eye. She was in a crisp, white kimono with a black belt circling her tiny waist.

It's her! Hélène sucked in her breath. She waved shyly, but Sylvie was too busy flipping her opponents to notice. Pedaling away, Hélène turned back a final time. Her instructor now held a robust man in a headlock. Hélène caught her breath.

Sweetness mingled with danger. She checked her arms for goose bumps.

❖

Hélène reached for the butcher knife. *It's not just for me*, she reminded herself. *It's good for him too.* She rolled up her sleeves and started chopping. Soon, clumps of carrot tops littered the counters. Chaussette, her kitty, slid in piles of whole-wheat flour as she tried to cross the floor on all fours. Instead of scolding her, Hélène sat on the ground to watch. As Chaussette pranced joyfully in the powder, Hélène's mind drifted back to the ninja goddess in the park. She had never thought uniforms could be so sexy. Sure, she caught herself looking at cops, and even sometimes...

Her eyes went back to Chaussette. The fuzzy cat became a novice figure skater struggling to stay upright. Hélène chuckled at her antics, imagining the chubby kitty in tights and a leotard.

That looks like fun. She jumped up. *I think I'll join you.* Soon, a frantic beat filled the kitchen as Hélène revved her body for action. Ditching her knife, she unleashed her feet. "Let's take over the linoleum!"

Chaussette observed her mistress with great interest. Attempting a fancy ballet move, Hélène slipped on the floor, creating a loud, ripping sound, followed by *"Mince!"*

After she had hit the floor, she glanced between her legs, giggling at the gaping hole. Black threads protruded, like spider legs. *Guess I'm not ready for the splits yet. At least, my jeans aren't.*

Hélène was still giggling on the linoleum when she heard a *slam.* Her face froze.

Wiggling to her knees, she adjusted her apron and grabbed the butcher knife.

❖

Chaussette ran off as soon as Marc strode into the kitchen.

"I'm starving," he announced, casting his coat onto a wooden chair. Mechanically, he pecked Hélène on the forehead. "Eww, you're dripping."

"Worked up a little sweat preparing dinner." Hélène smiled sheepishly.

Scowling, Marc wiped the sticky wetness off his lips with his handkerchief. "What's all this mess?" He gestured at the flour-dusted floor. His eyes fell on his supper: quiche Lorraine, grilled chicken, steamed squash, roasted potatoes, a healthy salad, and sparkling mineral water. "Humph," he grumbled, reaching for the radio. The news came on in French. He turned up the volume, grabbed a beer, and strode into the living room.

Lying on the sofa with his feet propped on a pillow, Marc clutched the *London Times*. Clearing his throat, he began reading with a heavy French accent: "Zer vas uh sliight differrance of opeenion…" The words came out choppy, mushy—like thick meat struck by blades in a blender.

"Dinner's ready," Hélène said in a discreet voice from the dining room.

Marc continued reciting in garbled English.

Hélène leaned over his prone body. "I said dinner's ready."

Grumbling, he opened a bottle of Bordeaux and poured himself a generous glass while Hélène served him a heaping plateful of quiche Lorraine, squash, and steamed potatoes.

Hélène sighed as she watched him chew while his eyes devoured his newspaper. She observed his square jaw mechanically rising and falling—gravitating from low to high speed—with each forkful. *That jaw...Efficient as an industrial sewing machine. And as appreciative too.*

Finally, she announced, "*Chéri*, I'd rather you not read the paper at dinner."

"I like to know what's going on," he retorted without raising his eyes.

"I'll tell you what's going on." She gravitated to his side of the table. "*C'est...*That's extremely rude!" She grabbed a fistful of his newspaper.

Marc gripped it defensively. She jerked hard; there was a loud rip.

Hélène flew backward and landed on the floor, clutching half the paper.

Marc shrugged and went back to reading his half of the article.

"Aaaiiee, that hurt." Hélène rubbed her lower back. From her view on the floor, he looked bigger, uglier. The stench of his athletic socks next to her nose made her stomach turn. *And those were on our living room pillows.* She shook her head. *He's such a pig.*

Then she glanced at her half of the paper.

"Since when do you read in English? You *hate* English."

Wincing, she poked her fork into her quiche Lorraine, which was just like her feelings toward her husband—stone cold.

Darn him. Everything's lost its flavor. As she chewed, Hélène tried to ignore the screeching sounds of race cars over an obnoxious TV announcer's voice. Chaussette sauntered back in and rubbed against her mistress's leg. Heavy purring sounds erupted from under the table.

Hélène smiled weakly. "*Bonsoir, bébé.* Maman will make you dinner as soon she's done, *d'accord*? At least *you* like what I fix for you!" She reached down to caress Chaussette's furry ears. Sitting on Marc's half of the torn newspaper, the cat's bushy tail camouflaged the headlines.

"Move, *bébé*, Maman wants to see something." Hélène gently pushed the cat away to read the title. "Mother kills eight-year old son with baseball bat." She cringed. "Yesterday, in Yorkshire, a thirty-eight-year-old mother killed her only child, an eight-year-old boy, with a baseball bat. She crushed his skull…"

Shuddering, Hélène shut her eyes. Marc's pale face appeared as he was reading this page. Not only was he pale, he was trembling. This thought made her feel queasy. *I shouldn't have been so hard on him. He's such a sensitive soul. And what did I do? I called him a pig! I'm such a beast.*

Under the title was a picture of the boy standing next to his mother. The boy was wearing a baseball uniform. They were both smiling at the camera.

Hélène continued, "…with his favorite bat on Monday afternoon, at approximately five p.m., at their residence in Yorkshire. The boy died instantly. As for a possible motive for the crime, it appears that rumors had reached his mother that…

"'Reached his mother that' *what*?…*What* rumors?" sputtered Hélène, holding up the ripped article. "Where's the rest of this?" Dropping to her knees, she dipped her head under the table.

A fluff of fur swayed before her, obscuring her vision.

"*Pousse-toi*, Chaussette!" She thrust her cat's tail from her face. Without knowing why exactly, Hélène desperately needed to know the rest of the story.

CHAPTER ELEVEN

Hélène tweaked her cat's ear playfully. "Breakfast time, *ma petite*," she whispered. Chaussette took a satisfying stretch, then followed her mistress to the kitchen as she did every morning. Hélène smiled at the pitter-patter of delicate kitty paws crossing the tiles behind her.

As the coffee percolated, she stretched her legs against the kitchen counter and let out a yawn. *I'm so glad it's Saturday.* She entered the dining room with two breakfast trays.

Guess he's eating by himself, she decided, digging into her cereal. As she sipped her herbal tea, she made a face. A sour odor entered her nostrils. "What's wrong with this chamomile?"

Then she saw the vase before her, full of wilting, yellow daisies. *It's time for you to go.*

Just then, Chaussette, lying in Hélène's lap, perked up her ears. Heavy footsteps followed. Marc wandered into the dining room, wearing one of his flashy Saturday morning sports outfits.

When he opened his mouth to yawn, a belch popped out.

Bon appétit, thought Hélène, scrunching her nose. *No morning kiss needed today.*

Marc ran his fingers through his stringy hair and glared at Chaussette. The cat ran for cover.

He plopped in a chair and grabbed a slice of bread, fumbling with his knife as he spread Nutella chocolate over it.

All of a sudden, Marc looked around his plate, then under the table. His face grew red.

When his eyes met Hélène's, he started to say something but stopped. Instead, he downed his first cup of coffee. Before he could put his mug down, Hélène poured him another cup and slipped out of the room.

❖

Hélène reappeared in an old T-shirt and jeans, with freshly combed hair and light makeup. She pecked Marc on the cheek. "*Au revoir, chéri.*"

"Where do you think you're going?" Marc's eyebrows knitted as he scrutinized his wife clutching her bicycle helmet. "It's Saturday, remember? We're going to the market."

Hélène inhaled deeply. "I don't feel like it."

"You don't *feel* like it?" Marc's voice rose. "What's that supposed to mean?"

"I made you a list of things to buy." She thrust a piece of paper at him.

Instead of retorting with a furious reprimand, Marc swallowed his anger, mumbling like a child, "But we always go together on Saturdays." His eyes were pleading.

Hélène pressed her lips together, fighting the urge to give in. "I know, *chéri*, but today, I'm going to check out the shops—by myself. I need some alone time," she stammered, squeezing her hips for stability.

The hazel eyes stopped pleading. Their pupils contracted; a cool glare replaced their softness. His voice was rough. "*Ouais*, I get it. Do whatever you want."

Hélène's body relaxed; her husband hadn't changed after

all. It was easier to bounce off a hard, abrasive rock. "*Super.* See you later, then," she announced, pecking him on the cheek.

"*Mon Dieu*, you need a shave," she hollered, rubbing her face as she skipped toward the garage.

❖

After pedaling for fifteen minutes, Hélène stopped before a plastic neon sign, "Jimmy's Cuts," adorning a bright pink building. She pressed her nose to the window to take in the hair salon's familiar kitsch interior. The owner, Jimmy, referred to it as his original "faux macho" design. Clashing colors—pastel pink and blood-red burgundy—bounced off paisley walls, creating a vibrant palette to jolt the eyes of delicate customers or, worse yet, virgins of kitsch.

Two young male customers sat beside each other in pink swivel chairs, each with their preferred hairstylist. One stylist sat in a wheelchair, wearing a tight T-shirt exposing the rugged contours of his chest and solid biceps. The other stylist was tall with broad shoulders, a square, stubbly chin, and a distinct Mediterranean nose.

Hélène paused before opening the door. She always felt out of place, given the stark contrast between her plain appearance and the salon's décor, the stylists, and the trendy clientele. For years, she fought against these self-conscious thoughts, even when Jimmy sent her home with a friendly kiss and freshly coiffed hair.

But today, Hélène felt different. She worked up a confident smile and squeezed past the heavy door. As it opened, funky music straight from the seventies boogied its way into her ears. As soon as they caught sight of her, the two hairstylists, Paul and Ramon, stopped snipping.

"*Ma chérie!*" Paul hollered, sitting up straight in his

adjustable wheelchair. Even though he was twenty-six, he still had a baby face, milky skin, fine blond hair, and huge chestnut eyes that appeared as if they had just been lacquered. All his customers—both men and women—fell under his spell. The fact that his ears stuck out like butterfly wings only added to his charm.

"Look what the wind blew in. *Salut, ma puce*," gushed Ramon in a thick Castilian accent. Ramon Gutierrez came from Madrid and was two years older than his boyfriend/colleague, Paul. His gorgeous dark brown hair and eyes blended perfectly with his tan skin. Rectangular, red glasses sat firmly over his sturdy nose; they matched his glittery red jacket, part of his eccentric clothes collection in honor of his idol, Elton John. A lone diamond shimmered from his left earlobe.

Hélène did her best to act cool as she waltzed over to the stylists. "*Salut, les mecs.*"

The two men planted kisses on her cheeks.

"Jimmy!" belted Paul. Within seconds, the owner of the salon appeared behind Hélène. Pursing his lips, he smacked exaggerated kisses into the air. "Darling! What a surprise! How's my favorite translator?"

Jimmy Black hailed from the outskirts of London. With reddish brown hair, cobalt blue eyes, Ivory soap skin, and a spray of freckles, he looked much younger than his forty years. His face was as clean-cut as a guy's could get, and his witty charm made him buddies with all his clients.

Hélène smiled at her old friend, who sported faded army pants and a bright rainbow shirt. She adored his accent in French, the way he modified her language with his own British twist—sprinkling it with original sayings. Now, at least, he had fully mastered it, not at all like when they first met, twenty years ago, at translation school.

"I'm desperately in need of a haircut," Hélène stated self-consciously.

"You're telling me." Jimmy winced as he ran his fingers through her windblown hair. "Hate to say it, but this mop looks like used cardboard, it's so frayed. What in God's name have you been up to? Never mind. We'll fix it, doll."

Jimmy grinned, lifting the freckles across his cheeks. "Where's your hubby?"

"At home."

Pouting, Jimmy crossed his arms. "But you always go to the market on Satur—"

"I decided to come to town on my own. He can do the shopping by himself—for once."

Jimmy lifted an eyebrow. "How daring of you, my dear. You're *so* right. Stagnation's to be avoided at all costs." He shook his head. A slight crack erupted in his neck. "Right."

Wincing, his hand went to his neck. "It's healthy to switch channels once in a while."

Hélène snickered. "You'd know about that, wouldn't you, Jimmy?"

"I wasn't cut out to be a translator, Hélène. You know that as well as—"

"You're right. You'd hate my job." The thought of him twiddling his thumbs at her desk, piled high with dictionaries, made Hélène chuckle.

Jimmy winked at her. "Let me tell you, woman, you'd hate mine too."

Hélène glanced at Paul and Ramon, who were busy snipping tufts of hair off their clients' scalps. "Probably. I'd be awful—I have absolutely no creativity."

"Don't say that, honey. *Everyone* can be creative. What about all those poems you're concocting?"

Hélène blushed. "They're just for me. They don't count. If I mess up on a word or a phrase, it's no big deal. My little literary escapades can't ruin people's hair. Or their love lives."

"You've got a point, my dear." Jimmy nodded. "Before I get the hives from this mess, let's get to work on yours."

Hélène's eyes bulged. "My what?"

"Your hair, silly. What did you think I meant?" Jimmy smirked. "That is, unless—"

"My love life never changes. You know that, Jimmy. How's yours, by the way?"

"My what?"

"Ah, don't worry about our sweet boss!" Paul called out gingerly. "He's having the time of his life."

"Certainly is. *N'est-ce pas*, lover boy?" Ramon waved his scissors emphatically.

Jimmy cleared his throat. "Come on, gals. Back to work. We're supposed to focus on our customers, remember?"

Paul and Ramon frowned and went back to snipping.

"I'm proud of you, sweetie," said Jimmy, draping his arm around Hélène. "Those mandatory Saturday morning excursions with your hubby to the market were tedious, weren't they? Good riddance."

He leaned closer to analyze her face. "That's not the only thing you tossed, is it? You seem different."

Hélène peered at him nervously.

"No, really. Don't take me wrong, honey, but…" Jimmy clicked his tongue. "It's like you got an upgrade. Despite that scary nest on your shoulders, you look good. Younger or something. New glasses?"

Hélène bit her lip. "*Non.* But I've lost some weight. I'm biking to work now."

"You rock, baby!" Jimmy wrapped a fuchsia frock around

his client. "I had no idea you were an athlete. I even feel a hint of muscle. Right here." He tweaked her bicep.

Giggling, Hélène jerked her arm away. "You kidding? I'm no athlete. It's just that the doctor said I—"

"Doctor? Oh, I hate doctors. You'll never get me near a hospital. I swear, I'd rather…Hmm, what have we here?" Jimmy twisted a blond strand around his finger, then held it to his nose. "You changed your shampoo! What's this cheap brand? Reeks like some sort of disinfectant. I told you never to sacrifice quality for—"

"Chlorine. You see, I'm—"

Like a toy, he swiftly twirled Hélène in her chair, frowning as he scrutinized her locks.

"So, sugar, same cut as usual?"

Hélène shook her head. "*Non*. For once, I agree with you. Stagnation's no longer an option. Let's try something totally new." She flashed him a brave smile.

"What a novel idea! Modifying *Madame*'s looks after nearly two decades," Jimmy quipped. "Normally, I would jump and clap my feet, but since I'm already forty," he brought his hand to his forehead, "it's safer just to faint!"

"Such a drama queen," Paul snickered as his boss hit the floor with a theatrical thud.

❖

"So when are you bringing your hubby to the salon?"

Hélène glanced up. "What?"

"Don't you think it's time you introduced us?" asked Jimmy, rinsing Hélène's hair. "Or is it too soon? I mean, it's only been twenty years."

Hélène shut her eyes tightly, searching for an excuse, but

came up with nothing convincing. Finally, she murmured, "I don't think he's your type."

The red-haired stylist squeezed shampoo on Hélène's scalp. "Honey, you mean we're not *his* type."

"Jimmy! I'm waterlogged!" moaned Hélène, trying to keep her nose above the flooding sink.

"Sorry, love." Jimmy cut the tap and lifted Hélène's head. Water streamed off her fuchsia frock, trickling onto her jeans. She wiggled uncomfortably. *Just what I need, wet pants.*

Jimmy whistled as he combed out her tangles. "So, what should we do with these precious locks?" He rubbed some strands between his fingers. "At least we got rid of the cardboard effect. That's a start. Now what, love?"

Hélène felt her heart skip. An adventurous thrill crept under her skin. "Let's do something completely *wild*."

"Wild you want, *wild* it is," Jimmy purred, aiming his scissors at Hélène's scalp. "But seriously, I've been cutting your locks for two decades. You've never once let me snip off a hair more than—"

"I'm so sick of this." Grabbing a handful of hair, Hélène flashed a disgusted look at the mirror. "It's so outdated. Like my life. So stagnant. Doesn't this remind you of a wilted flower?"

"More like a stale piece of bread," offered Jimmy with a chuckle.

"Make me younger. And less *bookwormy*."

Jimmy brushed a stray strand from her face. "Fasten your seat belt!" he ordered, hacking away at Hélène's head. "That hubby of yours won't know what hit him!"

CHAPTER TWELVE

The noon sun remained high in the sky—a rarity in Belgium. At the marketplace, vendors belted out their cheapest prices while clusters of shoppers scurried over cobblestones to snatch summer sale prices. Young couples pushed strollers laden with newborn babies; elderly gentlemen—in compact hats to conceal musty, greasy hair—clasped their wives by the elbows, anxious to escort them past pricey stands; children raced around stacks of multicolored vegetables.

The enticing aroma of free-range roasted chickens dripping on spits enticed shoppers to return home to satisfy their ravenous stomachs.

Like all Saturday market shoppers— a blend of *Bruxellois*, Eurocrat expats, and immigrants from faraway lands—Sylvie rushed around the stands before the market shut down. When she finally reached the flower stand, she realized her heart was fluttering under her tie-dyed T-shirt. It hadn't fluttered like this for ages. She began to sweat as her dark eyes scanned the rows of plants, flowers, and trees, searching...

A man in a flashy sports outfit was heading toward the other side of the market. He was jerking a grocery cart over the cobblestones. He seemed angry. She watched him until he reached the café and sat down at an empty outside table. She took a last look around the flower stand, then headed in the flashy sportsman's direction. Weaving through the thinning crowd of shoppers, she scanned each of the stands. But her eyes kept going back to the man. His head was cocked backward as he guzzled his beer.

It's him all right. Her fingers gravitated to her throat, suddenly as dry as the Sahara.

❖

Hélène checked her phone for the fifth time in ten minutes. *Still nothing.* Sighing, her eyes diverted from the wilting daisies on the table, settling on two plates piled with plump tuna sandwiches. Her stomach growled.

She squinted at a pair of furry ears protruding behind the dining table. "*Bébé*, where do you think he is?"

Her cat—comfortably settled in Marc's chair—replied with a yawn.

"That's not very helpful, Chaussette." Hélène's voice was tense. "Where do you think he is?" This prompted a "maaad" meow sound.

"Ah." Hélène searched her cat's eyes for confirmation. "So you think he's mad at me." She picked up her sandwich. "*Enfin*, too bad for him. I'm starving."

As Hélène chewed, she played with the alfalfa sprouts dangling off the bread crust. *Dangling tangles...tangling dangles...dangles?* "I'm getting just as bad as Jimmy." She chuckled, recalling the hairstylist's witty puns. "Speaking of tangles, how do you like my new do?" She twisted a few strands of her shorter hair.

Chaussette meowed.

"I'll take that as a compliment." Hélène shut her eyes and

rolled back her thoughts to a few hours before. Vivid images appeared at once.

Beaming with joy, she had sprung out of Jimmy's Cuts. Her new hairstyle was the epitome of modernity—short, voluminous, and glistening with silky cranberry highlights. Jimmy, Paul, Ramon, and their customers had stood gaping as she waltzed down the street, hair swishing like an actress in a fancy shampoo commercial. As she mounted her bike, Paul blew her kisses and Jimmy growled like a wild dog: "Grrr! Grrr! You go, girlfriend!"

Hélène smiled as she remembered her *coiffeur*'s remark. Then she glanced at her cat, which was getting dangerously close to her sandwich. "Nice decoration you've got there, *bébé*," she said, giggling as she plucked sprouts from Chaussette's whiskers.

❖

Sylvie's stomach gurgled as she pushed down her toes. As usual, it was a balancing act—one hand on the handlebars, the other grasping her camera, dangling from her neck. And now, her stomach was gurgling. *Just what I needed, indigestion.*

Her thoughts kept returning to the man at the market café.

There he had sat, in his flashy sports outfit, slurping his beer. When she had approached his table, his phone had rung. His chiseled cheeks blushed as he whispered into the receiver. She only caught a few words, but she could tell from the way he had stroked his mustache that he was flirting on the phone.

Is that Hélène on the other end? she wondered. He didn't seem to notice her standing nearby. He had simply ordered another beer, made kissing noises into the receiver, and then hung up.

As she approached the park, the latent sunlight filtering its rays through the trees projected delicate shadows before her. Whenever she saw something intriguing, Sylvie always held her breath. Grasping the camera as she pedaled, she recorded her images of couples snoozing in the park, migrants' legs winding over lovers' hips, tousled hair draped over picnic blankets, the sleepy faces of babies nestling in their parents' arms. If she could get some outstanding shots this afternoon, she just might complete *Art in Motion,* the title of her current project.

After an hour of shooting, she stopped to admire the pale stripes in the sky. A pair of distant planes crossed, attempting to erase each other's lines. Sylvie's hand went to her belly. Like most Saturday afternoons, the time went too fast. She was always so absorbed and, before she knew it, she had shot her five rolls of film. Obeying her rumbling stomach, she pedaled straight toward the Greek restaurant.

Familiar aromas greeted Sylvie as she entered Dionysos Taverna, filling her nostrils with the savory aroma of home. Before she could recognize the spices in the air, Vassilios—cradling four plates loaded with steaming food—waltzed over and planted a kiss on her cheek. Sylvie checked out the sumptuous dishes until her eyes landed on a youthful Greek woman sitting on a stool.

"Fancy meeting you here," Sylvie exclaimed in Greek as she sauntered to the bar. The woman looked up from her glass of retsina and intercepted Sylvie's friendly wink. *She's sure looking good*, thought Sylvie, admiring the way the woman's wheat-colored cashmere sweater set off her dark golden skin. Sylvie's eyes drifted over the tight, white jeans on the stool. As usual, the fabric molded its owner's body magnificently.

"Thought I'd drop by to see how you're doing. It's been ages," said the woman, nudging Sylvie's arm. As Sylvie kissed her olive cheeks, she inhaled the distinctive scent of lavender soap and fresh flowers. She murmured in Greek, "I'm so glad you did. I've really missed you, Aphrodite."

The two mademoiselles lost no time catching up with each other's news. As usual, Sylvie paid no attention to the male eyes fixed in her direction. Between sentences, she took an occasional bite from her *mezé* and a sip of retsina. At one point, the women laughed so hard, they had to grasp each other to keep from falling off their stools. Tears came to their eyes as they brought up the same quirky stories from their childhood in Santorini.

Vassilios—juggling plates and carafes of wine—joined them when he had a spare moment. As soon as Sylvie had polished off just enough retsina, he wrapped his arm around her neck and, before she could protest, seized her camera.

"Smile, you gorgeous goddesses," he said. Sylvie's arm was around Aphrodite's waist, while Aphrodite's arm was draped over Sylvie's shoulder.

"What the?" said Sylvie, startled. But before she could protest, he snapped the shutter, capturing the two women gazing with pleasure into each other's gleaming Mediterranean eyes.

❖

Hélène stared at the lavish window display for five full minutes. The shop was so elegant and so unbearably expensive, she had never had the courage to go in—until now. Each time she had approached the door, a price tag had caught her eye, sending a danger signal—freezing her foot in midair. *Pricey petals indeed.* She knew only too well what would happen.

If I even brought home one miserable leaf from this exclusive flower boutique, he'd massacre me and use the flowers for my funeral. She gulped at the thought of Marc ripping apart her purchases and flinging their contents—petal by petal—over the fresh soil of her grave.

If he were to shed a tear, it would be for the funeral expenses, not her.

Instead of lingering on that grisly thought, Hélène pushed open the door. Once inside, the intricate floral aromas calmed her mind while stimulating her senses. As she tiptoed around gold, bronze, silver, and crystal vases, she caressed the distinct blossoms, examining the hues of their petals, ingesting their unique scents.

Like Alice in Wonderland, Hélène was lost in a marvelous world of fantasy. *I must select the very best ones,* she decided. Whenever she approached a vase, she snatched a stem. If it didn't smell heavenly, she uttered, "Humph!" and moved on to the next variety. She soon emerged from the boutique with a gigantic bouquet bursting with three dozen precious flowers. Beaming, she floated down the sidewalk with her bouquet and walked straight into a...

"*Mince, pardonnez-moi!*" she apologized with a friendly wave to the tree.

Hastily crossing the street, she entered a chic boutique draped with a pink banner: "All Articles 50% Off."

Hélène stood inside, pondering the worn buckles on her boots. Just as she was about to sneak away, three elegant, constipated-looking salesclerks in pointy heels blocked her exit. In unison, they pinched their rouge lips, staring at her through their designer glasses—from the cranberry tips of her hair to the gummy soles of her boots.

Their smirks made Hélène cringe. *Show time!* Under their scrutinizing eyes, she dropped her fancy bouquet and raced around the shop, ransacking the place. She plucked designer suits, sailor outfits, and sexy dresses—all that fed her fancy—

from the priciest racks. The flabbergasted clerks kept clear of Hélène's path, lest she—in her ungracious haste—flatten them to the floor, trip over their spikes, or rip out their faux diamond earrings with a hanger.

At last, arms brimming with silky garments, Hélène sauntered out of a stall. *Get a load of this.* Winking at the witches, she waltzed to the cash register, trailing flamboyant fabrics in her wake. She burst out of the boutique with her bouquet and multiple bulky packages, fleeing the snobby salesclerks huddled at the door, fluttering their gloved fingers at her. The tallest cast out a squeaky "*Merci, Madame.* Come back to visit us soon!" A gust of glove-smothered, lip-stifling giggles ensued.

I'd love to reply with something nasty, Hélène mused as she piled her purchases onto her bike. *But why bother?*

Halfway home, she passed a tourist bus. Clutching her precious flowers to her chest, she waved at its overseas passengers and let out a triumphant war whoop.

❖

"On the house." Vassilios plopped another huge carafe of retsina on the counter.

"*Ah non,* I can't. I'm driving." Sylvie shook her head.

"You came by bike, Syl." Vassilios topped off her glass.

"Actually, I was going to swim a few laps. Then I have to develop these." She tapped her camera.

"What an exhilarating Saturday night, little cousin. It's time you take a few lessons in romanti—"

"Leave her alone," interjected Aphrodite. Then she softened her voice. "Honey, what happened to—"

Sylvie frowned. "Let's not even go there."

"But at least she—"

"Was a tyrant." Sylvie took a deep swig of retsina.

Vassilios put his arm around her shoulder. "Come on, she wasn't that bad. Sure, she wasn't as sweet as you, hon. Nobody is."

Muffled ringing sounds erupted from Sylvie's backpack.

"Speak of the devil," continued Vassilios. Before Sylvie could stop him, he fished her cell phone out of the front pocket. "Here."

Sylvie glanced at the number. "Perfect timing, Lydia. Back you go..." Before she could stuff it in her backpack, Vassilios grabbed the phone.

"Sylvie's secretary speaking," he gushed into the receiver. "Lydia, is that you? Of course, darling. She's right here." He winked at Sylvie and passed her the phone.

"*Allô? Non*, that was Vassilios. From Dionysos Taverna, the Greek—*Oui*, the restaurant. *Non, non*. The waiter." Blood rushed to Sylvie's cheeks. She glared at Vassilios. "Anyway, never mind. What did you...What? My place? Tonight?" Sylvie's back stiffened. She shook her head. *No way. No bloody way.* "*Non*, that's impossible. I have to—"

Vassilios grabbed the phone. "Lydia? It's Vassilios. She'd *love* to."

Sylvie scrambled over the hairy waiter to retrieve her phone. Before she could stop him, he added, "*Super*, I'll tell her. You two have a delightful evening," and hung up. Smirking, he handed Sylvie the phone. "Wasn't so hard, was it?"

Sylvie's nostrils flared. "I can't believe you just—"

"Honey, next time, try to sound a bit more enthusiastic." Vassilios wiped a stray hair from Sylvie's chocolate eyes. "You don't want to give the wrong impression, *n'est-ce pas*?"

"I can't believe you just did that, Vassilios," Sylvie said coldly.

Aphrodite nodded. "I'd be pretty upset if I were you, Syl."

"Of all the rotten tricks, you—"

"What's done is done, my sweet cousin." Crossing his muscular arms, the waiter faced her smugly. "You've got exactly one hour to get home, throw on some sexy clothes, and whip up a batch of your knockout ouzo cocktails."

"But I was going swim—"

"Syl, your laps can wait." Vassilios flashed the women his sexiest macho smile. "Besides, I thought you liked cross-training."

When Aphrodite shot him a quizzical look, he placed his hand on her thigh. "Just another kind of workout, my dear," he explained with a wink.

"You're so wicked, Vassilios," said Sylvie, concealing a nervous chortle. Before she could protest any further, he bumped her off her stool and marched her out the door.

As she was biking away, she heard a loud, "Wait!"

Out of breath, Vassilios thrust her camera at her. "You might need this!" he added with a naughty glimmer in his eye.

❖

Up to her ears in packages, Hélène fumbled with the key to open the front door. As soon as she entered the house, something fuzzy rubbed against her ankles. Then the purring began.

"Shh, *bébé*. We need to be quiet right now." Setting her purchases down, she poked her head into the living room, where a soccer match was blaring from the TV. Socked feet were protruding from the sofa. Hélène sneaked a peek over the top. There sat Marc in his latest Adidas sportswear, fast asleep, clutching a can of beer to his chest.

He'd never treat a baby as well as his booze, she thought, watching the can rise and fall with each nasally induced breath. Sighing, she tiptoed around the sofa. *Some things never change.*

She started to rescue the tipping beer can but stopped her fingers midair. Her nostrils whiffed a mixture of stale sweat and suds from a musty brewery. The stench was so offensive it nearly propelled her from the room.

What a pig! Hélène recoiled from her husband, plugging her nose. She switched off the TV, grabbed her bags, and escaped up the stairs, with Chaussette in tow.

Safe in her bedroom, she stuffed her purchases into her closet, except the bouquet and a small black shopping bag. "Come on, *bébé*, it's show time." She raced toward the bathroom. Chaussette, recognizing the curtain call, jumped on the counter for a first-row seat. The bathroom's tiles soothed the soles of Hélène's overheated feet. Her toes curled in delight as she set her sumptuous bouquet on the counter. Chaussette promptly licked a yellow petal.

"You haven't seen anything yet." Hélène swept her locks with a pink brush. Then she dabbed on face powder, topping it off with pink lipstick, hairstyling gel, and a spray of perfume. Her eyes were gleaming as she reached into the elegant shopping bag. Counting to three, she pulled out the precious garment. Its black silkiness flowed through her fingers like smooth lava. She nestled the delicate fabric against her face. *Délicieux. Like a forbidden fruit.*

Peeling off her old clothes—like a banana shedding its skin—she turned to face the mirror. Except for her white cotton underwear, she was nude. Ever so gently, she ran her fingers over her thighs. *Much firmer.* She smiled inwardly. *All that biking, swimming, and dieting seems to be working.* Taking a deep breath, as if plunging underwater, she resurfaced in a sexy black dress. Hélène gasped. Another woman was staring back at her.

Her hand went to her mouth. So did the woman's. She crinkled her nose. So did the woman.

The new dress was a bit tight, revealing shapes that Hélène, only weeks before, could never have dreamed of. As she inspected her curvy hips, she felt so light, so sexy…

Her imagination took over. Grabbing her toothbrush, she whispered, "Ladies and gentlemen, that's all for tonight. Thank you for coming to Broadway!" She pursed her cherry lips in mock humbleness. "It's been such a gratifying role—dutiful housewife transformed into a sexy bombshell…In a matter of seconds!"

The blond woman in the mirror gushed with pleasure. Her cheeks turned rosy pink as she clutched her bouquet of flowers, bowing deeply to the audience, each time revealing a more succulent view of her ample neckline.

Hélène's heart was racing under her new dress. After a discreet pause, the fans became ecstatic. Chaussette, purring loudly, thumped her tail on the counter in applause.

"I'm off to the gym…I'll be back for dinner!" Marc's brusque voice traveled up the staircase, hitting Hélène like a water balloon in the face. Her thoughts skidded back to earth. Instead of luscious bouquets and extraordinary Broadway reviews, her thoughts flashed back to the sweaty odors emanating from her husband's sportswear.

She scratched her head. "Wait!" she hollered. "Didn't you already go to the gym?" No reply. She tried again, louder: "Marc! Can't you hear me? I said—"

A door slammed. "Never mind," she muttered, shrugging. "Maybe the workout will get rid of some of that tension of his…"

The woman in the mirror shrugged back, but this time, with a frown. *Tension?*

Hélène looked at her ample breasts in her new, sexy dress. *Could it be sexual tension?* The idea made her nipples harden. She felt the skin tingling on her back. *Non, that's ridiculous.* The woman in the mirror licked her lips provocatively.

Feeling her blood rising, Hélène clenched her fists. *I'm the one who's ridiculous. Get me out of this before I tear it to pieces!* Forcing the delicate dress over her head, she felt a snag.

Hélène pulled harder. There was a loud, ripping sound. Freed from the silky garment, she balled it up like a wad of used Kleenex and stuffed it into a bathroom drawer.

❖

Sylvie's mind was racing as she sped toward her apartment. While waiting at a traffic light, her thoughts went back to Lydia. Under her sweatshirt, she felt a familiar twitch. She glanced at her arms. Goose bumps. *Non, non, non...I'm not letting her get to me this time.*

Ahead were two teenage girls with their arms linked. As they skipped down the sidewalk, they were pinching each other, laughing hysterically. She observed the pair as she rode by.

No wonder we broke up. We never even enjoyed each other's company. She felt a bitter taste in her mouth. *So who am I trying to kid? We're not "just friends"...*

"We're enemies!" she hissed as a surge of adrenaline pushed her feet hard on the pedals. Drops of sweat streamed from her face as she climbed the final hill.

Twenty minutes later, Goldie rubbed her whiskers against

her mistress's fuzzy slippers. Standing at the kitchen sink, Sylvie peered at her honey-colored cat. *"Désolée, ma puce. I've been ignoring you."* She reached down to caress her pet, whose glistening eyes begged affection. "You must be starving. Maman got you something tasty at the market today. A nice, fresh piece of sushi. They took the seaweed off, just for you."

Sylvie unwrapped a generous portion of raw fish and plopped it in Goldie's dish. "So I spoil you a bit. Why not? You deserve it, *ma petite...*" Her voice trailed off as the cat's tiny head bobbed. Intense licking noises ensued. "Guess you don't need chopsticks, eh, *bébé?*"

Within minutes, Sylvie was humming to the Greek music blaring in her living room. *I shouldn't be in such a good mood,* she decided. *Not tonight.* The thought of Lydia's impending arrival put a quick halt to her humming. She extracted more vegetables from her backpack. The carrots smelled like sweet dirt. She waved them in the air like a policewoman directing traffic, then tossed them in the sink.

Grabbing a pair of scissors, she picked up her bouquet of yellow marigolds, trimmed their stems, and plopped them into a water-filled vase. "Drink up, it's on the house."

Next, after washing a bagful of vegetables, she dropped the scrubber, stuffed her hands in her apron, and leaned against the sink. "Where do you think Hélène was today, Goldie?" she asked her pet, who was busy scraping bits of sushi off her whiskers with a paw.

"C'est bizarre. The florist said she didn't come by. But it's Saturday..." Despite the bits of sushi dangling from Goldie's face, she snatched up her cat. Ignoring the fishy odor, she nuzzled close and whispered into her tiny ear, "I've got an idea. Let's invite Hélène over for dinner sometime."

Goldie began purring.

"And I'm sure she'll like you too." Goldie rubbed her fishy face against Sylvie's T-shirt in agreement. Then the doorbell rang.

❖

Hélène felt better as she bounded down the stairs. Her old clothes were much more comfortable. When she entered the kitchen, she gasped at the shopping cart next to the refrigerator. Ever so cautiously, she peered into it. *He actually did the shopping.* She opened a brown paper bag. *With vegetables!*

But Hélène's mood dampened when she entered the dining room. Her week-old daisies greeted her with drooping yellow petals. The sour stench of the water made her pinch her nose as her mind spun a few verses of poetry.

These daisies are so full of grief,
Like choirboys before an angry priest.

She held the wilted daisies. "From now on, Chaussette, Maman is going to spoil us rotten with fancy flowers. Papa won't even notice the difference!" she declared to her kitty, shoving the flowers and old plastic vase into the trash. *We're turning over a new leaf!*

Hélène arranged her new, expensive flowers with gusto—she bent their stems at the waist, just like she had seen in Japanese *ikebana* magazines when she was young. As she toiled with the stems, her mind drifted back to those long afternoons with her mother in the library. She had been so curious, memorizing the different ways people arranged flowers, depending on their culture. But cut flowers were so pricey then, she had never had a chance to practice what she read in those marvelous, glossy books—until now. Her fingers knew exactly where to tuck and snip.

"*Voilà!*" she exclaimed, contemplating her masterpiece with tears in her eyes. *Why didn't we do this earlier?* Chaussette, who had fallen asleep in a dining room chair, woke and yawned.

❖

As soon as Sylvie opened the door, a syrupy scent filled the air, prompting her prominent nose to twitch. Stepping back in haste, she nearly tumbled over Goldie, who—instantly recognizing their visitor—ran for cover.

"What's with the apron?" smirked Lydia, smothered in fur. Waving her precious Hermès scarf, she narrowed her eyes to scrutinize Sylvie's appearance, starting with her wind-blown helmet hair. Then she scanned her muscular chest, rough-cut jeans, and fuzzy yellow slippers. Without waiting for a reply, she put her white silk pants into gear and barged into the room.

Sylvie stepped aside. *Better give the buffalo some roaming space.*

Lydia, oblivious to her French perfume's ambush effect, stood smacking her chewing gum. After a few seconds of impatient chewing, she blew a large bubble at her hostess. In a huff, she wiggled out of her coat and handed it to Sylvie. "Polite as ever, I see."

The bubble burst with a crisp pop. Lydia licked the gum off her teeth and cast a dirty look under a chair. "So it's still here."

"What?"

Lydia pursed her lipstick-caked lips. "That foul cat of yours."

Sylvie felt the hairs rising on her neck, but she forced herself to remain silent. Smiling stiffly, she clutched Lydia's fur coat, which was so cumbersome, she wondered if animal chunks still lurked inside. She headed toward the closet.

Just as she reached for a hanger, a pair of hands clasped around her hips and warm breath entered her ear. "Thanks for inviting me."

Sylvie stiffened.

Lydia's voice grew soft and sexy. "It's been such a long time."

Sylvie felt goose bumps erupting all over her body. She held her breath.

"Don't I get a kiss?" Lydia purred.

Sylvie threw the coat on a hanger, flipped around so fast that Lydia didn't have time to purse her lips, and fled across the living room. "You're hungry, I suppose?"

Frowning, Lydia headed toward the sofa. "*Ouais*. Starving, actually." She whipped out her cell phone. "Remember those soufflés? What's that French caterer's number?"

"Actually, I went shopping. I'm going to make some—"

"That's so cute of you, *ma chérie*. But let's get real here. If you want to impress me, *eh bien*, we both know how." Licking her lips, Lydia wiped her hand on her brow. "Ooh, it's getting so warm in here," she said, squirming on the sofa. "*Mon lapin*, come here. I miss you already," she groaned, forcing her knees together and dropping the phone.

"Open a window, then," was the reply from the kitchen. "I'm busy making—"

"Get real, Sylvie! We both know you suck in the kitchen." Lydia burst into laughter. "Get it? You suck. *Ah…oui*. You suck…" She drooled, caressing her own breasts. She grimaced with passion as her nipples hardened.

Sylvie came out of the kitchen sporting a scowl. Lydia reeled in her wandering fingers and tapped a cushiony spot next to her. "That was rude of me, pumpkin. *Désolée*. Let me make it up to you," she pleaded in her most saccharine voice.

Sylvie contemplated the long, red nails tapping her sofa. She pressed her lips together to control her rage. Feeling a headache coming on, she inhaled to reduce the mounting tension—not only in her head but in other, more intimate parts of her body.

❖

What goes with a sumptuous, healthy supper? Hélène asked herself while slicing endless red bell peppers. *Un peu de musique...* She sashayed over to the radio. Cutting off an obnoxiously loud football announcer, she settled on a trendy pop song. Instantly, her bare feet ignited the linoleum while her hips twisted to the tunes. After a few minutes, she started cutting a red onion, just as a love song came on. Its gentle rhythm and poetic words brought a cascade of hot tears down her flushed cheeks. She continued slicing until she could barely see. Setting down her chopping knife, she approached the wilted daisies in the trash.

"I'm sorry, my friends. That was so insensitive of me." Sniffing, she retrieved the faded, plastic vase. Fresh tears flooded the corners of her eyes. She brought her face to the opening of the vase. There was some fusty liquid still inside, with a yellow daisy floating on its surface. But before Hélène could rescue the tiny flower, her vision grew fuzzy. She reached for the nearest chair as her head began to spin.

❖

Sylvie wiped her hands on her apron and approached the sofa. Instead of sitting next to Lydia, however, she ducked under the coffee table. "Come to Maman, *bébé*."

Goldie, normally docile, kicked at Sylvie's arms as if her mistress were going to roast her on a spit. Chuckling, Sylvie hung the kitty—four paws dangling, claws extended—over Lydia's fake platinum curls. "Mind watching her while I make dinner?"

Lydia yelped. "Watch out for my trousers! They're raw silk. One hundred percent natural, from—"

"Be right back." Sylvie dropped Goldie next to Lydia. The cat hissed at the older woman, provoking a loud yelp, then scrambled under the table.

"*Tu vois*, she still likes you." Sylvie winked. "Must be your charm."

"It's not like I'm allergic or anything," muttered Lydia, wiping the perspiration off her forehead. "It's just that…I prefer dogs." She sighed, clutching her white silk handkerchief.

"*Non*. You hate dogs."

"*Eh bien*." Lydia glanced at the fish bowl on the table. Two goldfish were swimming circles around each other. "*D'accord*. Fish, then."

Sylvie chuckled. *This is hilarious.* "You hate fish too."

As Lydia scanned the apartment, her eyebrows rose at all the plants she had never cared to notice. As if in a jungle, dozens of varieties seemed to be dangling their branches at her from assorted pots filling the room. "*Eh bien*, plants are—"

"Come on, Lydia. You hate plants." Sylvie contemplated the pout on her former girlfriend's dainty lips. *She hates everything I love*, thought Sylvie, stiffening. *How come I never realized this before?*

❖

Hélène lowered her head. Instantly, her eyelids dropped, and she began to daydream…

The two women are in the swimming pool. Sylvie's arms grasp Hélène, who is lying facedown in the water, coordinating her breathing as she practices the crawl. All is going smoothly until Hélène takes in a mouthful of water. Abruptly, she stands, coughing. Her face is red.

"Ca va?" asks Sylvie, tapping her on the back. Hélène nods. But as soon as she catches her breath, she flies into a rage.

"I'm never going to learn how to swim! Did you see that? I can't even breathe without swallowing half of the pool. I'm such a loser!" She spits water out of her mouth and flings her diving mask across the pool. "I'm just wasting my time and yours too," she gasps, flailing her hands. Sylvie shoots Hélène an encouraging look; then she takes off toward the other end of the pool. Hélène concentrates on her teacher's legs swishing rhythmically under the surface. Marveling at how swiftly they propel Sylvie through the water, she forgets her own angst—until she loses sight of her teacher. Minutes seem to tick by, yet Sylvie remains underwater. Hélène shifts her weight from one foot to the other. The pressure mounts in her ears, pounding in unison with her heartbeat, accelerating with each passing second.

❖

Sylvie softened her gaze. Something was different about Lydia tonight; she seemed almost vulnerable. *Maybe it's the lighting?* Glancing up, she noticed that one of the fluorescent bulbs was out, directly above their heads. *Or maybe it's something else? She almost seems afraid—as if the sofa were about to swallow her body and all her elegant clothes. She couldn't be afraid of me, could she?*

Sylvie smiled inwardly at this idea. Straightening her back, she shoved her hands in her pockets. "You don't like dogs, cats, plants, or fish." She cleared her throat. "*Alors,* Lydia. What *do* you like?"

The older blond woman wiggled uncomfortably until she spotted the bookcase behind her, which took up the entire wall. "Books?" she squeaked through pursed lips.

"You don't even read."

"But I do." Lydia's eyes scanned the wooden shelves. "I mean, I did. They're all in the garage now."

"You don't have a garage."

"So what? You've made your point." Lydia's voice sharpened. "So I'm not a literary genius like you. And I couldn't care less about all those stupid living creatures. That is, except for..." She flashed a wicked smile and grabbed Sylvie's thigh.

"Hey, lay off!" Sylvie swiped Lydia's hand away.

"So you want to get rough with me, eh?" Lydia got up, unzipped her sweater, and flung it on the sofa. "Fine with me, *mon lapin.* Just tell me the rules." She took a bold step forward.

Sylvie felt her ex-girlfriend's fingers caressing her cheek, igniting a spark in her groin. She backed up slowly. Her leg hit the table. Goldie ran under a chair.

"Ah, forget the rules. We won't stick to them anyway. *N'est-ce pas, mon lapin?*" Lydia squealed, lacing her arms around Sylvie's neck and pressing her face against her strong chest.

Contemplating the delicate nose crushed between her breasts, Sylvie couldn't decide whether to push her ex-lover away or hug her back. Within seconds, she realized she didn't have a choice.

❖

Hélène's daydream in the kitchen intensified.

Something shoots out of the water at Hélène's side. It's Sylvie. Her swim teacher shakes her head—flinging water in Hélène's face—rips off her goggles, and gasps for air. Her muscular chest rises and falls rapidly; her mouth, still gaping, forms a weary grin as she holds up her hand triumphantly.

Hélène chokes back tears as she reaches for her mask. I'm such a coward, she decides, pursing her lips as hot tears roll down her cheeks.

Sylvie gently wraps her in her arms.

Hélène nearly collapses at the touch of Sylvie's strong body against hers. Her warmth penetrates right through Hélène as if melting through her skin, straight to her core. Hélène's legs seemed propped up as if on stilts. She stands wavering and whimpering like a child.

Sylvie tightens her grasp around her until she calms down. Taking her face into her hands, she whispers, "You're not a loser, Hélène. And you're sure not wasting your time. Nor mine. You've come a long way, bébé." To seal her words, Sylvie kisses Hélène gently on both cheeks.

Hélène stops crying. She gazes into Sylvie's glistening, toffee-colored eyes. Mon Dieu. Hélène's eyes widen. She feels the pressure mounting until the flooded gates to her heart burst open; a torrent of emotions fills her veins. She shuts her eyes to keep them in place.

Sylvie takes this as an invitation. With a swift burst of confidence, she targets Hélène's lips and leans in…

❖

"Aaahhhh!" cried Lydia, jerking her head back. Pressing her palms against Sylvie's T-shirt, she pushed her away. "You're disgusting!"

"That's hardly polite." Sylvie grimaced. Lydia's words had just doused the flame in her jeans.

"But…" Lydia contorted her face. "You are. You *stink*!"

How could I have forgotten that unique talent of hers? That priceless lack of tact she exhibits so effortlessly? remembered Sylvie, smiling rebelliously. "How sweet of you, Lydia. *Vas-y*, let me have it. If insults are how you get your thrills—"

"*Non*, I'm not kidding. You really stink, Sylvie. Your boobs smell like…fish!"

Sylvie chuckled. *This is better than a cold shower.* "Sushi, actually."

Lydia's eyes bulged. "Sushi, my ass. Don't try to lay that one on me."

"Come on, Lydia."

"You can't stand sushi, remember? All those raw, wiggly, squishy…" She carved circles in the air with her long, red fingernails.

Sylvie's eyes followed her ex-lover's fingers, which she noticed were laden with even more diamonds.

"You're right. I hate sushi."

Lydia's voice was squeaking. "So you didn't eat sushi?"

"*Non*." Sylvie smiled. *This is starting to get fun.*

"Or any kind of fish?"

"*Non*."

"You bitch! You cheated on me!" Lydia pulled her hand out of orbit and aimed it at Sylvie's face, but Sylvie ducked. Lydia began slapping Sylvie on the back.

As Sylvie took the blows, the words of her karate teacher came to mind: "*Attention*: your hands are weapons.

Never hit anyone unless it's in legitimate self-defense." She wondered if this counted. All those painful months after their separation—not to mention all those painful months during their relationship—and now, all the pain Lydia was inflicting on her.

The muscles in her abdomen tightened. *I can't take this much longer…*

❖

Splayed over the kitchen table, Hélène's hair fanned over her face like bunches of wilted daisy petals. The napping position was terribly uncomfortable, but she was enjoying her daydream too much to care.

Then the phone rang. She woke with a start and stumbled her way into the living room. Her heart was still pounding from the romantic scene in the pool.

"*Allô?*" she grunted, plopping on the sofa. "Aaaiiee!" *What the heck?*

She slid her hand under her buttocks and pulled up an empty—now flattened—beer can.

"Are you all right, *ma chérie?*" asked a concerned voice on the phone.

Hélène smiled at the Flemish accent. "Mathilde!" she replied as she cleared crumpled newspapers and empty beer cans from the sofa.

"*Je ne te dérange pas?*"

"*Non*, you're not interrupting anything. I was just…" *In the middle of the wildest dream.* Hélène rubbed her sleepy eyes. "Getting comfortable. What's up, Mattie? Which exciting country are you in now?" Knowing how lengthy her friend's têtes-à-têtes could get, she propped up her feet and settled in for a long conversation.

❖

Sylvie took the rainfall of punches remarkably well. In fact, she was surprised to notice her body tingling in ways that weren't purely painful; something familiar arose—something she remembered liking. *But you hate her,* she told herself. *She's your enemy, remember?* When the familiar warmth snuck between her thighs, however, all Sylvie could think of was: *Mon Dieu, it's been a long time.* Normally, she would have weighed the pros and cons of her actions. But tonight, her body was begging her to postpone all forms of internal discussion in this complicated situation: *Who cares? I'll worry about it later.*

She proceeded to block Lydia's subsequent blows with her favorite karate moves. In a flash, she grabbed her opponent's forearms. Squeezing them like a vise, Sylvie fixed her eyes on Lydia's wide, glistening pupils. Adrenaline rushed through her system, heightening her senses. Like a famished lion on a mountain summit, she mentally licked her chops while anticipating her next meal. As she moved in for the kill, nostrils flaring, she was surprised to feel less resistance from her victim. Instead, Lydia's sudsy voice slid into her ear like a slippery bar of soap: "*Ah, mon lapin.* I knew you'd come around…"

❖

Mathilde sat like a queen, propped against a pile of fluffy white pillows on her luxurious, king-sized bed. With her curly black hair draped over her shoulders, her cream-colored silk blouse—tucked into a tight black miniskirt—enhanced the softness of her ebony skin.

"Which country? I'm back in boring Belgium. *Enfin.*" Mathilde sighed. "But what about you? What was that 'aaaiiiee' I just heard?" The Congolese-Belgian woman began applying a coat of cherry-colored polish to her toenails. As soon as she leaned over, her blouse's deep neckline revealed a generous portion of bosom.

"Just a minor accident with one of Marc's beer cans."

Mathilde flexed her feet in panic. "What? Don't tell me he hit you—"

"*Non*, not at all," Hélène countered. "You know Marc. He always forgets to pick up after himself."

"You mean he's still a slob."

"I didn't say that." Hélène wrinkled her nose.

"But he is. Anyway, you sound funny. Have you been crying?"

Hélène's thoughts swept back to her daydream. *Have I?* She touched the corner of her eye. It was moist. Then she remembered tears running down her cheeks in her dream. "*Non*," she lied, wiping her eye. "Just making dinner."

Mathilde pointed her freshly painted toenail at Silly Milly, her white poodle, dressed impeccably in a matching silk outfit. Crumpled like a tiny ball, the dog sniffed the nail and gave a delicate pooch sneeze.

"*Dis-moi*, Hélène. You can't hide things from me. Marc's been yelling at you again."

"*Non*, Mathilde, I swear. It's the onions. He's not even here, he's at the gym."

"What for? Those puny muscles of his? Anyway, forget him. What are your plans for tonight?"

"Nothing special. *Pourquoi?*"

"I've got a fantastic idea." Mathilde began applying nail polish to her other set of toes. "This new restaurant just opened in my neighborhood and...guess what?" Her voice rose a notch. "Drum roll…Tonight's Ladies' Night! We get two meals for one. Cool, non? *Alors*—"

"Sorry, Mattie. I already made dinner."

"*Très bien.* You're a great homemaker—and an excellent translator. Now be a good girl and stick it in the freezer. I've got the address right here and—"

"If Antwerp were only closer—"

Mathilde whistled. "It's not like I'm inviting you to the Congo," she insisted, referring to her mother's African origins. She began brushing her poodle furiously with a silver brush.

"I was planning on finishing my latest poem and—"

"Listen to me, sister. You've got your whole life to churn out those flowery poems of yours." Mathilde wrapped a silk ribbon around Silly Milly's poodle head, then kissed her.

"But I—"

"Come on." Mathilde jumped. Sucking in her stomach, she beamed at her full breasts and ample posterior in the mirror. "I don't look anywhere near forty. And neither do you!"

"That's sweet, Mattie. But like I said, I was planning to—"

"It's Saturday night. We're young, beautiful, and hot! Let's go get us some *action*." Mathilde reached into a drawer, pulled out a BiFi sausage, spread her generous lips, and inserted half of it into her mouth.

Exiting the bedroom, Sylvie slid her slippered feet over the hardwood floors. "I'll make us some tea," she called over her shoulder. She felt aches in her limbs after all that effort. *It sure has been a while.*

"Whatever you want, *mon lapin*," came Lydia's reply, muffled between the sheets.

Entering the living room, Sylvie felt compelled to tiptoe over to the large bay windows. A breeze was blowing outside; the trees across the street swayed in unison. *Ca alors, it's already dark outside.* Two trees, intricately intertwined, seemed to be dancing together. Sylvie squinted at the silhouettes formed by their branches. Images of her family at local neighborhood festivals in Santorini came to mind. *Yaya used to...*

Her reminiscence was interrupted when a familiar voice erupted from her bedroom. "Come back in here, *ma chérie.* I'm lonely."

Mince! I forgot about her. As she pried her eyes away from the dancing limbs outside, something pinched in her heart. As soon as her feet hit the cold kitchen tiles, she had an adverse physical reaction. Goldie, curled on her favorite kitchen chair, shot her mistress a look of concern.

"I'm sorry, *mon poussin*," she told her, scratching the kitty's neck. "She'll be gone soon."

"What did you say?" came a shrill voice from the bedroom.

"I promise," whispered Sylvie, gently caressing her pet's bristling orange fur.

Lydia repeated, "What did you say, *chérie?*"

"Let's have our tea in the living room!" Sylvie winked at Goldie as she began preparing the tea.

❖

Hélène caressed Chaussette, who had crawled onto her lap. "Sounds like a great plan, Mattie, but I'm exhausted tonight."

Mathilde bit into her sausage slowly, with her sensuous lips rolling over its smooth edges. "Exhausted? You just need to move your big derrière around some more," she mumbled.

"Hey, I've been dieting for over a month now, and biking, and swimming, and—" Hélène pinched the fat around her belly. *And it's working too.* She jiggled a leg in the air.

Mathilde yanked the sausage from her mouth and let out a whistle. "I'm in shock. What's gotten into you?" Admiring herself in the mirror, she added, "Girl, I've known you for twenty years. You *hate* sports. You don't even own a pair of shorts. Or tennis shoes."

"People can change, you know."

"So now you're a jock? I've got to see this."

Hélène's fingers clasped her biceps. *Firm, all right.* She squeezed the tiny wad. "I'm not exactly a jock, but—"

"Where do you swim?"

"At a pool nearby. I'm taking lessons every morning before work. That's why I've been so tired lately," replied Hélène, fiddling with Chaussette's tail.

"Why didn't you tell me? You know I love to swim! I could come before work. *C'est à dire…*When I'm in the country." Mathilde aimed the remaining half of her BiFi at her dog. The poodle sniffed at the sausage suspiciously, then licked the tip with her pointy pink tongue.

"But you see…"

Mathilde's voice swelled with excitement. "Wait…Who's taking the class? Any good prosp—"

"They're private lessons," Hélène interrupted. "And we start at seven in the morning."

"*Quoi?*" Mathilde's eyebrows shot up. She yanked the sausage out of Silly Milly's mouth and started nibbling on it. "Have you gone mad?"

"*Mais non.* I decided it was time to learn how to swim."

"Really? So you rise at dawn, to dip your derrière in some freezing pool? And then you decide to go on a diet, or whatever, and..." Mathilde waved her sausage in the air. "*Attends*, Hel. I'm not *that* stupid. So, what's his name?"

❖

Lydia sat on the sofa, fiddling with her hair. As her fingers teased her blond curls, her eyes skimmed over the black-and-white photos decorating the walls. Just as her eyelids began to droop with boredom, she spotted a colorful book on the coffee table: *Marigold Mountains.*

She opened the oversized book. Underneath a glossy photo of a field of yellow flowers, a dozen jagged sentences were written in old-fashioned calligraphy.

"Hmmph. Who reads poetry anyway? It's so pretentious!" she declared, loud enough for Sylvie to hear her in the kitchen. She flung the book onto the table and frowned at the volumes piled high on the bookshelves. The first time she came to Sylvie's apartment, she had been surprised to see the massive wooden bookcase, especially since nearly all the titles—the ones that weren't in Greek—were about plants and flowers, even the photography books.

Lydia smirked. Her past girlfriends had all been businesswomen, attorneys, or doctors. One had even been a gynecologist. They were rich, sexy, powerful...and proud of their social status. She had wondered right from the start what she was doing with an artist, or a jock, or whatever Sylvie was. And now, as she heard the Greek swimming instructor clinking around in the kitchen, Lydia's petite jaw tightened. "She's cute, but that's about it. The chick can't even cook. *C'est pathétique.*"

❖

"What's *whose* name?" asked Hélène, nearly dropping the phone.

"You tell me."

"What are you talking about?" Hélène's voice rose.

"People just don't change overnight, *chérie*, unless they've got a really good reason." Mathilde licked her half-eaten sausage. "And I bet I know yours: the big MLC."

"MLC? What's that?"

"Midlife crisis. *M'enfin*, Hel, don't you read *Cosmo*?"

"Well..."

"We all go through it." Mathilde smiled knowingly. "So tell me, what's he like?"

"I don't know what you mean, Mattie. My doctor's the one who told me—"

"Sure. 'Doctor's orders.' Good excuse."

Hélène's shoulders stiffened. "If you're insinuating that I'm with someone else, you're wrong. Marc is—"

Mathilde's full lips twitched. "Nice try, Hélène, but I don't buy it. You've been telling me for years that you're only interested in your husband. And that's your choice. *Mais franchement, ma chérie*, I'm finding this hard to believe."

Hélène sighed loudly. "But it's true."

"Okay. Don't get all upset, hon. Just for fun, then, what's your instructor like?"

"What instructor?"

"Your swimming instructor, silly. I can see him already. Tall, dark, and muscular?" Mathilde waved her sausage, then popped it into her mouth.

Hélène laughed. "Well...You got the tall, dark, and muscular part right."

"I *knew* it!" Mathilde thrust her hand into her cleavage. She caressed her boob as she chewed. "And he's got on a tight little swimsuit, *n'est-ce pas?* Tight, white. Right?"

"Tight, white, right, white...*Quoi?*" Hélène cocked her head. "What's white, and what's tight?"

"That's it, *ma chérie*. Tight and white."

"Ah, Mathilde, you're confusing me."

"I'm talking about his swimsuit. It's white, non? It's so white it's completely transparent. Which means that when he goes into the water..." She rubbed her chest harder. "*Ah oui, bébé!*" She stopped to catch her breath.

"Mattie..."

"It's so tight that it sticks to his skin, perfectly emphasizing his—"

Hélène's temples started pounding. "Stop it, Mattie!"

Mathilde plopped back on the bed. "Just because you want him all to yourself doesn't mean—"

"I hate to disappoint you, Mattie, but you've got it all wrong."

"*Ah, bon?* So he's fat and ugly, with carpet hair all over his back?"

Hélène squirmed at the idea. "Of course not!"

"*Très bien*, because I don't believe you for a second, girl." Mathilde resumed painting her dog's claws with cherry fingernail polish.

"Actually, my instructor's—"

A door slammed. Hélène stopped mid-sentence as soon as Marc's gym bag landed on the hall floor with a thump. When she jumped up, Chaussette slid off her belly, scrambling for cover. Hélène whispered, "*Désolée*, Mattie, I've gotta go."

❖

Sylvie emerged from the kitchen in a rainbow-colored apron. Setting her tea tray next to *Marigold Mountains*, she whispered, "I see you're enjoying my poetry books."

Lydia wrapped her arms around Sylvie's neck. "This one's so thrilling, I can't keep my hands off it. Just like I can't keep my hands—"

Sylvie untangled herself. "You're such a bad actress."

"You're wrong about that, *mon lapin*." Lydia shook her finger at Sylvie, who cringed at the long, bright pink nail glued to its tip.

"Actually, I've been told I'm rather talented," whispered Lydia in a sexy tone.

Sylvie's eyes opened wide as the fingernail carved pink spirals in the air.

"*En fait*, I can lie through my teeth, and you'd never know what hit you."

Sylvie's face went white. A flashback of Lydia—sitting in the very same spot just months before, explaining what had happened on her latest business trip—hit Sylvie like a slap in the face. The trip was only supposed to be for business, but...

"What do you expect? I'm only human," Lydia had declared flatly.

Some confession, Sylvie had thought at the time. That damaging moment had marked the end of their relationship. Until now.

What am I doing? The Greek athlete pondered Lydia's pretty face. It was always pouting, like a poodle begging for a snack. *Either I stay angry and single, or I give in and see what happens...*

"*Tu m'écoutes?* Are you even listening to me?" Lydia tapped Sylvie's muscular knee. "I can lie through my teeth, and you'd never—"

"Wanna bet?" said Sylvie, switching gears. She flashed Lydia a mischievous smirk.

"*Ouais*, let's bet." Lydia grinned.

"I'll go get Goldie. She's a great judge of character."

Lydia's lips trembled for a split second until she pinched them into a strained smile. "*Quelle bonne idée.* Where *is* that darling pussy of yours?"

❖

Hélène pointed a frying pan at her cat. "Let's do something romantic, *bébé.*"

Chaussette wagged her tail.

Why didn't I think of this before? Hélène wondered as she placed the dinner candles on the picnic table. It was an unusually warm evening for Belgium, even in summer, where rain was always lurking in the clouds, threatening to drizzle over the Belgians and their picnic plans.

Hélène aimed her eyes at the rare, cloudless sky. In minutes, the table was decked with her favorite checkered tablecloth, fancy fresh flowers, and tall, romantic, red candles. She ran her fingers through her shorter, bouncier hair.

Can't wait to see his reaction, she told herself, sprinting into the kitchen and emerging with plates of steaming food. At last, she removed her apron and lit the candles.

"*Chéri,* it's time for dinner," she called into the house. No response.

Hélène's eyes caught a slice of evening sun. She hollered again, a bit louder.

I could wait all evening. After all these years, I'm used to it. But the sun can't. She watched the yellow slice disappear as the sun exited the garden.

As if on cue, Marc made his appearance. Through the dimness, Hélène noticed her husband's sports clothes. His white sweatshirt took on a yellowish hue from the flickering candles. *C'est bizarre. What's he been doing all this time?* she wondered, only too aware of his penchant to shower and change before dinner. She frowned. *So much for romance.*

The couple stood in the backyard staring at each other.

Finally, Marc broke the silence. "Why are we eating out here?"

"Thought I'd surprise you, *chéri*. Look how beautiful our garden—"

"It's pitch dark. I can't see for beans."

Hélène replied cheerily, "But your nose still picks up fragrances, *n'est-ce pas*? Aren't the roses, the hyacinths, the lilies—"

"Whatever. I'm starving." Grabbing the nearest dish, Marc heaped piles of food onto his plate.

Hélène's face fell. Forcing a smile, she announced, "I made these dishes with the food you picked out at the market today, *chéri*."

"So what?" came the gruff reply.

Hélène squinted at her husband as he shoveled her creations into his mouth. Trying to shut out his chomping noises, she shifted her eyes to the luxurious bouquet in its new crystal vase. In the dark, the flowers seemed different— deformed, almost ugly. Her hand went to her scalp. *What if my hair looks like that?* she wondered, caressing its smooth contours. She bit her lip. *What have I done?*

❖

While Sylvie searched for Goldie, Lydia knocked back her tea like a shot of whisky. As she was pouring her second cup, Sylvie returned, cradling her disoriented pet in her arms.

"Sorry to wake you from your nap, *ma puce*. But it's time to bond with Auntie Lydia." Sylvie promptly dropped the cat onto her guest's lap. Lydia was nervous, but Goldie was worse. She had a complete fit. Forked over the Belgian woman's white silk pants, her claws dug deeply into their owner's thighs.

Stifling a scream, Lydia brought her fingernails around Goldie's neck. But instead of wringing it, her hand trembled as she tried to pet the cat, whispering in a faltering voice, "*Gentil petit chat*...Nice little kitty..."

Sylvie watched with amusement. "Say you love cats."

Lydia's eyes narrowed. She took a deep breath. "I love..." She stopped mid-sentence. "Something smells god-awful all of a sudden." She flashed Sylvie a sarcastic smile. "*Mon lapin*, have you been cooking again?"

Sylvie's thick eyebrows shot up.

"Did you stick something in the oven?" Lydia snorted as she poked Sylvie in the ribs. But she stopped poking when something wet and warm landed on her thigh. "*Beurk!*" she wailed as a brown, watery blob slid down her leg. "My silk pants! They're ruined!"

Before Lydia could fling Goldie across the room, Sylvie swooped up her pet. Holding Goldie at arm's length to protect her apron, she smiled broadly at her ex. "I'd say she's a pretty good lie detector, and," she winked at her cat, "you just failed the test."

Chapter Thirteen

The swimming pool area was empty except for a lone figure on the bench. Outside, the darkness was as thick as oil. Hints of streetlights flickered beyond the windows, like dying fireflies. All was quiet.

Sylvie rubbed the sleep from her eyes. She still wasn't used to getting up so early, especially on Monday mornings. She tried not to consider the other, more appetizing options: staying in bed, jogging in the park, or eating scrumptious breakfasts with Goldie on her balcony. These options seemed all the more tempting as she sat in her bathing suit, shivering on the bench.

Where is she? She glanced at the clock. It was already 7:07. She pulled her robe tightly against her chest, trying to trap warm air. The terry cloth felt soft against her bare skin, as comforting as a baby blanket. At last, she heard a noise. Swiveling around, she caught Hélène racing toward her.

Sylvie held up her hand. "*Attention.* No running, remember?"

Stopping abruptly, Hélène nearly stumbled. "*Désolée*, I forgot. I'm late and—"

"It's really dangerous," declared Sylvie, pointing to the sign. "Poolside rules."

❖

Hélène scrutinized the stern look on her instructor's face. Something seemed different. *Sure, I'm late. And yes, I broke the rules. But there's something else. I wonder what?* The more she looked at Sylvie, the more her features appeared hardened. *Maybe it's the lights.* She glanced at the fluorescent tubes hanging from the beams. *Go away*, she told her negative thoughts, stuck on her mind like a blouse clinging to a clammy back. *Hope it's not me.*

Just when Hélène started to apologize again, Sylvie's features softened. In a gentler tone, she said, "Sorry I scolded you, Hélène, but I am a lifeguard. That's part of my job." To Hélène's surprise, Sylvie leaned forward and gave her a kiss on the cheek.

Hélène returned the kiss, but stiffly. Her instructor's cheek was cold. Without knowing precisely why, something told her not to get too close.

"How was your weekend?" Sylvie asked as they entered the shallow end.

"Ah, just the usual. Cleaning, eating, shopping—"

"Did you see those new flowers at the market? The red ones with—"

Hélène shook her head. "I didn't go. Marc went alone. I figured he could help out with the chores for once. I'm always doing them."

"So that's why I didn't see you."

Hélène's eyebrows rose. She imagined Sylvie at the flower stand, spending her Saturday afternoon amidst sweet-smelling blossoms and glorious plants while Hélène was getting her hair chopped at the salon. She took a shallow breath, remembering her husband's reaction to her new hairstyle.

He had pointed his finger at her. "You looked better before. Before all that stupid dieting and exercising. That doctor's full of—"

Hélène had crossed her arms. "May I remind you that I'm doing all this for medical reasons?"

"Don't try to tell me medical reasons made you ruin your hair!"

Something snapped in Hélène. "*Ca suffit!* Enough!" she had shouted, facing him squarely.

Her thoughts jumped back to the pool as Sylvie thrust a kicking board into her hands. "You must have a mind-blowing imagination since you're such a prolific poet, so let's pretend it's Monday morning and you're at your swimming lesson, okay? Time to put your face in the water, *Madame*, and start kicking."

She's like a captain at sea, barking orders to her swab. Blushing, Hélène complied with her captain's orders by donning her mask and gently lowering her head into the cool water. *Sure, I'll play along. If I'm your swab, you've got to tell me when and how you want me…to wet your decks.* Once her face submerged, Hélène caught a glance of her swimming instructor's muscular thighs. How different she felt with Sylvie, compared to Marc. It was only Monday morning, but she could already sense that these private lessons were becoming the highlight of her week. The realization was both scary and confusing. Her lips began to tremble.

❖

After the early-morning lesson, Hélène's legs propelled her bike forward like a powerful machine. She noticed the difference in her speed as her tires flew over the cobblestones. For once, her body had more than enough energy to obey her mind's orders. After another fruitful swimming workout, she was on top of the world.

When she stopped at a red light, she caught her reflection in a shop window. Her new sports outfit narrowed her waist and gave definition to her slimmer thighs. The only drawback was her hair. As usual, it was stuffed—more like wadded—into her helmet. It reminded her of her conversation with Sylvie, fifteen minutes earlier.

After the workout, Sylvie had entered the locker room and approached her. "I like your haircut. It's cute."

Hélène had flashed her a puzzled look. "Did you say something?" she had asked shyly, turning off the dryer.

"I like your hair. It's cute like that," repeated Sylvie. Hélène couldn't remember the last time anyone had used the word "cute" to describe her or any of her attributes. She had blushed, turned on the dryer again, and wished she could blow herself and her new haircut out of the locker room.

A car honked nearby, yanking Hélène from her thoughts. "*Eh*, Eddy Merckx, get a move on!" a man yelled as he drove past in his black Mercedes. Hélène stuck her tongue out at him.

"Why don't you try cycling, *imbécile!*" she called out as she pedaled through the green light.

Minutes later, when she trotted inside her office building, for the first time in her life, she felt light on her feet—*just like an athlete!*

❖

Sylvie did a few more leisurely laps and then got out of the pool. *Goldie's probably starving by now*, she realized, grabbing her robe. Within a half hour, she was home for her favorite part of early-morning workouts—pigging out at breakfast.

Goldie sat perched on a chair, her tail swishing with excitement as her mistress—legs propped on the balcony rail—dug into a huge bowl of muesli.

"Who do you think it's from?" Sylvie pointed to an envelope with her spoon. Goldie meowed. Sylvie's eyes lit up. *She loves getting news from home as much as I do*, she mused, glancing at the tiny Greek letters printed on the back of the envelope that had just arrived.

"You're right, *bébé*," she said, ripping it open with her spoon. "Let's see what news Mama has this time."

❖

Once in the ladies' room, Hélène dove straight into a stall. A few seconds later, she emerged in front of the mirror. "*C'est beau!*" she cooed, fingering the fabric of her new outfit. Her silk blouse, with its deep neckline, subtly revealed the contours of her firm chest. She spun around. Her new, tight black pants emphasized the slimmer contours of her buttocks. *All this exercising is worth it. And I love these new clothes. Who said money can't buy happiness?* She splashed water on her face. The coolness soothed her hot cheeks.

After drying her face, she pulled her brush through her hair. Abruptly, she stopped. Her eyes darted from her new, shorter haircut to the oversized brush in her hand. She stared at the one thousand-pronged styling device, remembering the day her great aunt had given it to her as a communion gift. *I was so excited because it was my favorite color: fuchsia. How old was I then?* Her eyelashes fluttered. *Twelve. Good riddance!*

After chucking the brush into the trash, she stuck her hand under the faucet and ran her fingers through her hair. *Much better.* Next, she began powdering her face, until beige clumps of coagulated powder congregated on her rosy cheeks. She gasped. *Quel horreur! I can't believe I've spent the past two decades caking this crap on my face.*

With a huff, she promptly tossed her powder case into the trash.

❖

Sylvie read each sentence ever so carefully, taking in her mother's words as if they had been written in gold. She adored Mama's letters, even though they made her homesick. Her mother had a special talent for arranging words. They went straight to her daughter's heart. As Sylvie read each line, she imagined Mama standing on the porch of their home, talking to her.

Halfway through the letter, however, Sylvie's face fell.

Goldie offered her mistress a concerned meow.

Sylvie forced herself to continue reading. After ingesting all of Mama's precious words, she folded the letter into tiny squares and stuffed it in her pocket. She shivered at the cool breeze passing through her thin cotton T-shirt. Squinting past her balcony, she looked over the trees and tall buildings blocking her view of Brussels. A dark cloud emerged in the sky. She watched it grow bigger, pondering Mama's words until the cloud masked all the blue. She swept a tear from her eye and went inside.

"Please be home," she pleaded into the phone. After four rings, Mama picked up.

Sylvie's voice cracked. "Mama? It's me. I...I just got your letter," she stammered, choking back her tears. "I'm so sorry. What do you want me to do?"

❖

At least I still have these, Hélène reassured herself as she smeared red lipstick over her lips. Then she heard a snap. She held up the metallic part of her lipstick, but somehow, the red had disappeared. She looked down and gasped; it had smashed headfirst on the slippery tiles. It looked like just an injured beetle. She poked it with her boot to see if was suffering.

After so many years, Hélène's lipstick knew the contours of her mouth better than her husband did. *But that's not hard. When was the last time he grazed my lips with his mustache?* She couldn't remember. What had happened to those blissful days when they were just two goofy students fumbling around? She was unable to rummage up the sensation of his lips on hers. Maybe her sensorial memory was numb. Or maybe Marc needed glasses, for he always aimed his kisses four inches above the target. Hélène pursed her lips. *It's always the forehead deal: Tight. Quick. Dry. And right before a meal.*

To squash these depressing thoughts, Hélène lifted her foot and aimed her heel at the red blob on the floor. *Time to put the stunned thing out of its misery.*

Then she remembered her new leather boots. *Non. Not in these. Someone else will have to do the dirty deed.* With a triumphant flick of her wrist, she chucked her metallic lipstick holder into the trash. Next came the light-blue eye shadow. Then the trusty nose drops. Her eyes glistened as she tossed the items over her head; each entered the trash with a "plunk."

"Two points!" she exclaimed, fishing through her makeup bag for more ammo. After salvaging her mascara, she contemplated the empty makeup bag. *Marc's mother gave this to me, and it was so expensive. I couldn't possibly...* Then a wicked smile took over her lips. *Oh, yes, I can.* She chucked the tacky bag into the bin.

With a triumphant smile, Hélène applied her remaining weapon—light brown mascara. "*Voilà.* Done." She looked at her watch. "In one minute flat." *A record.* Her mind did the math: it usually took her twenty minutes to apply makeup, twice a day. *Multiply that by twenty years and...I don't even want to know how much time I've wasted.* She shook off the depressing thought. *Who cares? Time to start living in the present.*

Donning her glasses, Hélène sped out the door. As she rounded a corner, she ran straight into Jérôme, a sales colleague who reminded Hélène of an asparagus, he was so pale and thin.

"*Mon Dieu!*" Jérôme called out, right before Hélène crashed into him. The pair keeled backward and landed on the floor, with Hélène on top.

"Brilliant way to say good morning, *ma chère collègue,*" said Jérôme in the suave voice he mastered to sweet-talk his clients.

"Sorry," stammered Hélène, pushing away from the young man's bony chest.

But Jérôme had another idea; he wrapped his arms firmly around her waist. "No problem!"

"I was late and—" Hélène pushed harder against his chest.

"No need for apologies, *chérie.*" Jérôme winked. "Your method works better than caffeine—what a jolt!" he exclaimed, peering into her blouse.

"If you don't let me off you this instant, I'll teach you what a real *jolt* is, Jérôme!" spat Hélène, ducking under his elbow.

❖

Sylvie hung up the phone. As if on cue, Goldie hopped into her lap. Sylvie smoothed the fur over her collar, exposing "Marigold" embroidered in Greek letters on its yellow strap.

"Remember when Yaya made this for you, *ma puce*?" The cat gave a slight nod. "Last Christmas, when…" Sylvie's voice trailed off. "Mama doesn't want me to go home, Goldie, but I feel so useless here. What should I do?" She wiped away the tears dripping down her cheeks. Goldie's green eyes widened. She rubbed her moist nose against Sylvie's finger.

"You're right. I'll do what she says and stay here with you." She frowned, contemplating the thought. Then her face perked up. "Let's write Yaya a letter. Maybe it will make her get better." She gently removed her cat from her lap. "We'll send her some pictures too. She loves portraits of you, Goldie." *Since you're the closest thing I've got to giving her a great-grandchild.*

❖

As Hélène read the words out loud, her tapping fingers could hardly keep up. She was obsessed with finishing the translation before lunch. She figured that the faster she read the words from the source language, English, the faster she would type into the target language, French. In theory, this was true, but in practice, it wasn't. Every few words she made a mistake. Sighing, she stared at the screen: "This lifting operation is done mechanically with a starting handle and a winch to completely clear away the straw, which falls freely from the…"

Abruptly, she stopped. *C'est ridicule. Who cares?* She brought her coffee cup to her lips. Her tongue dove in, fishing for the sweet Arabica taste that had occupied the cup for two decades. But for the fifth time this morning, all her tongue caught was air.

This isn't fair. My brain needs this stuff to function.

She frowned as she typed: "I am so sick of translating this crap. What's the use anyway? Who cares about winches?"

Leaning back, she gazed at her painting of Santorini. A chubby cat was napping on a white wall draped with plump red flowers. An olive-skinned woman stood next to the cat. An emerald sea with delicate white-tipped waves lurked behind the pair. A lone seagull flew overhead. Where the blue sky met the sea, soft yellow lines arched from the sun, raking the water's surface.

Hélène stared hard at the painting, imagining the sun's warmth on her fingers. She heard the seagull's cry piercing through the waves lapping in her ears. Her nose sensed the sea salt trapped in the cracks of the wall, lingering in the folds of the woman's simple dress.

She shut her eyes, treasuring these images, marveling at the Greek painter's talent.

Why am I sitting here, suffering with my boring translations? I'd have more inspiration over there, on that island. How I'd rather be there right now...

To her surprise, a new image appeared: Sylvie was standing in the ocean, beaming.

Hélène held her breath as her instructor's muscular body, enhanced by her wet bathing suit, hijacked her imagination.

Why can't I be like her? So exotic and full of life, so sensuous...

A loud ringing interrupted Hélène's thoughts.

"*Salut*, Cecile," she said into the phone. "Ah, because it's always you at noon. Besides, who else calls me? Who? You've got to be kidding, Ceci. He's way too busy. Can't even find time to call me, let alone take me to lunch. But who cares? I've got you, *n'est-ce pas?*"

Ignoring her colleague's ensuing monologue about Marc's

rudeness, and how she should dump him, Hélène cradled her painting of Santorini. With the tip of her finger, she stroked the cat's painted fur and smoothed the ridges of the woman's dark, curly hair.

At last, Cecile stopped ranting about Marc. She brought up a more pressing topic: her rumbling stomach.

"Okay, give me *deux minutes*." After hanging up, Hélène winked at the Santorini woman.

"See you after lunch. By the way, how do you say '*bon appétit*' in Greek?"

❖

Cecile tapped her fingernails impatiently on the picnic table. Then she spotted her colleague inching through the grass behind the office.

"About time, Hel, I'm starving."

"Nice to see you too, *chérie*." Hélène plopped on the bench.

Cecile unwrapped her *jambon* baguette sandwich. Before inserting it into her mouth, she uttered, "I've been meaning to ask you something."

Hélène emitted a nervous cough.

"Everyone's wondering. I mean, they've been asking me, 'cause I'm your best friend and all. And, of course, I should know." Cecile flipped her hair. "*Enfin*, it's just that…What have you been doing lately? You've completely changed, *ma puce*."

"I lost some weight." Hélène sank her teeth into a whole-wheat sandwich overflowing with dark greens.

"It's not only that." Cecile shook her head. "You seem so much happier. More carefree."

Hélène's eyes glistened. "Well, I—"

"They gave you drugs at the hospital, *non*?" Cecile brought her baguette to her lips.

"Drugs?" Hélène shook her head vehemently. "*Non*. I just have to be careful what I eat."

Cecile sputtered as she chewed. "*Ouais*, but—"

"See? I'm eating more healthily." Hélène pulled some alfalfa sprouts from her sandwich. When she dangled the sprouts in the air, Cecile scrunched her dainty nose.

"It was hard at first, especially cutting out the sugar, but I got used to it. I might sound like a TV commercial, but it's true.

"Your loss!" Hélène added, gobbling the sprouts. "Now I've got way more energy than before. I swear."

Cecile opened a thermos. "So it's not drugs." She poured herself a large mug of coffee. "Speaking of energy, this will make you fly!" She thrust the thermos at Hélène, who blocked it with her hand.

"I'm an herbal-tea-with-honey gal now." Hélène dropped a red *églantier* teabag in her mug.

"*Beurk*, looks like blood," gasped Cecile, peering at the bright red water.

"Well, it *does* improve circulation. Try some!" Hélène held her mug under Cecile's nose.

Cecile pushed it away. "*Non*, thanks. I need my daily caffeine fixes. But it's true, Hélène, you look great. More natural. More confident. Your face has this healthy glow...I wish I were as disciplined as you, but I just can't give up all of my naughty little habits." Lowering her thick lashes, she gave Hélène a slow wink. "And speaking of naughty little—"

"But it's easy, Ceci. Just add more fresh fruits and vegetables to your—"

Cecile waved her napkin. "Listen, *chérie*, I wasn't going

to mention this, but since I'm your best friend, I'm going to anyway. There's a rumor going around..."

Hélène's eyes widened. "Tell me, Cecile," she asked gravely, leaning forward.

❖

Time for a break, Sylvie decided. She had already given four swimming lessons, with two more to go. She slicked her moist hair back with her fingers, slid on her jogging suit, and left the pool.

Ten minutes later she entered her favorite hangout between lessons: a local bookshop stocked with used books from all over the globe. She loved the invigorating feeling that hit her every time she entered the shop. The books piled high over all four walls roused her senses as the familiar odors hit her nostrils: ancient printing presses, dusty pages, fresh India ink, even the tangy sweat fabricated by excess literary creativity. Her imagination conjured up images of writers of all kinds: those suffering, others celebrating triumphs, famous ones from faraway lands, or budding novices yet to be acclaimed.

As usual, she made a beeline to the *Arts et Nature* section. While leafing through stacks of colorful hardbacks filled with poetry, she noticed a young woman in the nearby gay/lesbian section. The woman, wearing a cotton T-shirt loosely tucked into a tight pair of jeans, was leaning against a wall with her long legs crossed, staring straight at her.

Sylvie glanced at the woman's leather cowboy boots. *That seals the deal—she's family all right.* The youthful swimming coach forced herself to keep her eyes on her poetry books, even as she felt the jean-clad woman's eyes inspecting every inch of her body.

Sylvie's heart was pounding under her jogging suit. Half

of her begged to acknowledge the other woman's presence, while the other half desperately fought the urge.

Ah, non. I came in here for a book, not another girlfriend.

❖

Cecile's eyes darted around the picnic table. "Okay, but don't say I'm the one who spilled the beans."

Hélène felt tiny hairs rise on her arm. She nodded.

Cecile whispered, "People are saying things about you."

Hélène frowned. "That's what rumors are, Cecile. You don't have to give me the definition. I've got enough dictionaries in my office to—"

"They say you've got *un amant.*"

"*Quoi?* A lover? That's ridiculous!" gasped Hélène. A chill spread through her body.

"That's why you look so good."

Hélène shook her head in disbelief. "What in the—"

"I'm your best friend, so I should've been the first to know, *non*?" Cecile pouted. "Let's be honest. I've never kept secrets from you, Hel. Ever since we—"

"Wait a sec." Hélène adjusted her glasses. "I can't believe you think—"

Cecile began carving into the pine table with her fingernail. "Why didn't you tell me?" she stammered.

"But I don't have anything to—"

"Maybe I'm not your best friend anymore." Cecile raised her head. "Ever since you fainted, you've changed." Her voice grew louder. "And we're not just talking about your diet!"

Hélène reached for her hand, but Cecile pulled it away.

"*M'enfin*, Ceci, you *are* my best friend. Would I lie to you? Everything's fine with Marc. You know I'm not the type."

"I know." Cecile finished carving the letter *C* and began

carving an *E*. "Never mind. It's just what everyone's saying, especially the guys. Like Jérôme. They all think you're so cute now, with your new hairdo and fancy clothes." Her voice trailed off.

"Seriously?" Hélène lifted an eyebrow.

Cecile fluttered her eyelashes at Hélène's new silk blouse, which perfectly accentuated her ample bust. "Seriously."

"No kidding."

"And they're right, Hel. Don't take me wrong, but you *are* much prettier without all that makeup. *Une beauté naturelle.*"

Hélène felt her cheeks blush.

"Let's see. Take off your glasses." Cecile held out her hand.

"Whatever for?" Hélène waited for an answer. When none came, she set her glasses on the table and wondered what was coming next.

❖

Sylvie snuck a glance in her direction. Sure enough, the young woman's gaze was aimed straight at the tight, muscular buttocks lurking under Sylvie's jogging suit. *Figures.* The swimming instructor began to sweat, recalling only too well that all of her past girlfriends had focused on her buttocks before asking her out.

"That's what you get for being a jock," Lydia had said when the topic surfaced on their first date. "A butt like yours is worth its weight in gold, and double that when you're wearing jeans."

Sylvie blushed, remembering what had happened after that. *Good thing I'm wearing sweats today. If I ignore her, maybe she'll go away.*

As soon as Sylvie kneeled to examine the books on the

bottom shelf, footsteps approached her from behind. She grabbed the first book she saw. On page fifty-four, she saw a glossy photo of a tree surrounded by a brown pile of mud, titled *Capturing manure with the naked eye.*

The footsteps stopped directly behind her. Sylvie stiffened.

"Naked eye?" whispered the woman in a sexy voice. "Cool."

The woman kneeled next to her. Sylvie flipped the page. The space between their bodies grew smaller. Sylvie could feel her earlobes growing hot. The woman's perfume had a honey-like aroma that made Sylvie dizzy it was so sweet. She glanced at the woman's attractive face and awkwardly stood.

The young woman stood as well. She smiled at Sylvie and leaned closer, which made Sylvie feel even dizzier. She noticed the younger woman's teeth—only inches from her own—perfectly white and straight, and her luscious brown eyes with long, silky eyelashes.

Sylvie felt hungry all of a sudden. *Should've had lunch,* she decided, peering into the mouth-watering eyes. *What was I thinking?*

❖

Cecile nodded enthusiastically. "Much better."

"What's much better?" Hélène squinted in her friend's direction.

"I can finally see your eyes, now that all that blue gunk is gone."

Hélène blushed. "*Merci,*" she mumbled, reaching for her glasses. "I think." She glanced away. "If only Marc thought the same. He hates my new look."

Cecile's jaw dropped. "No way. He should be thrilled." Her eyes hovered over her friend's deep neckline and the smooth, sexy dimple between her breasts. "Anyway, who cares? Men never say what they think. We just have to judge them by their actions."

"That's what I was afraid of. You're depressing me, Ceci." Hélène bit into her sandwich.

"Come on, *chérie*. Don't be so coy. Your man can't keep his hands off you, can he?" retorted Cecile with a loud slurp of coffee.

Hélène nearly choked as she chewed. "Are you joking? Those hands have never been farther away. They're either holding a pencil, a newspaper, a remote control, a dumbbell," she took a frustrated pause, "or a can of booze."

Contrary to her nature, Cecile was speechless.

"And he hasn't stopped criticizing me since I lost weight and bought my new clothes. It's so frustrating!" To illustrate her point, Hélène waved her sandwich, flinging its contents. Alfalfa sprouts and a cherry tomato landed on Cecile's plate.

"Good idea. Let it all out!" encouraged Cecile, popping the tomato into her mouth.

❖

The two women in the bookstore stood unusually close to each other as they introduced themselves. In the tension-filled air, created by the proximity of two people noticeably attracted to each other, this was no minor feat.

Sylvie learned that the woman was getting her master's degree in women's studies. The woman made a point of informing Sylvie that her university was just around the corner. Then she scribbled her phone number on a piece of paper and handed it to Sylvie. Their hands touched for a brief moment as she took it.

"Call me," said the woman, fluttering her long eyelashes.

She turned to leave, hesitated, and swung around. "By the way, I moved out of the dorm last year."

She winked at Sylvie and turned on her boot heels.

Flattered and confused, Sylvie shook her head. *I really should've had lunch*, she mused as the young woman's perfectly molded derrière marched its way out of the store.

❖

"*Très bien.*" Cecile gave Hélène a pat on the hand. "Now that you've had your little veggie tantrum, let's get down to business. I want you to listen carefully to what I have to say."

Noting the unusual graveness in her friend's voice, Hélène nodded solemnly.

Cecile looked straight into her eyes. "You say everything's fine with Marc, *eh*? Well, that's the *wrong* answer, *ma fille*. It's time I put you straight."

"Spare me the details, Ceci," blurted Hélène.

Cecile shook her head. "You need to hear this." She took a sip of coffee. "Have you ever considered he's…*eh bien*, to put it crudely, bangin' someone else?"

Just then, a skinny girl in her early twenties with funky dark glasses joined their table. Her outfit looked like a uniform straight out of a Girl Scouts catalogue from the sixties. Her fake blond pigtails shook when she plopped on the bench next to Cecile. In a squeaky voice, she uttered, "Ahh, sounds juicy. Who's bangin' who?"

Cecile cast her a dirty look. "Stay out of this, Therese."

Hélène ignored the intrusion. "He'd never do that, Cecile. He's the faithful type."

"That's what I thought about my last husband, right before our divorce. Remember?"

Therese stopped slurping her soda. "Let's get this straight.

Your husband was bangin' someone else, *eh*, Cecile? And yours too, Hélène?"

"I *said* stay out of this, Therese." Cecile leaned toward Hélène. "*Ma chérie*, listen to me. I've been through this. Let me give you some precious advice. When he comes home at night, you've got to inspect his clothes for clues. You know, go through his suit pockets. Look for anything suspicious: traces of lipstick, perfume, blond hair."

"*Attention!*" Therese slammed down her soda. "I resent that. Blondes aren't the only ones stealing husbands."

"*Calme-toi*," barked Cecile, inspecting her colleague's pigtails. "I was talking about *real* blondes." Chuckling, she turned to Hélène. "Go through his pockets."

"You're such a witch! You're...just jealous." Therese aimed her peanut butter sandwich at her colleague's face.

"Butt out, Therese," Cecile continued.

"*Très bien*," retorted the girl, grabbing her sandwich and storming off.

Once the Girl Scout uniform was across the yard, Cecile whispered, "You deserve to know the truth. Even if it hurts. What's wrong with him, anyway? Why would he want you to stay ugly?"

Hélène's face fell when she heard this. Averting her best friend's eyes, she focused on her half-eaten sandwich, trying to hide her trembling hands.

After an uncomfortable pause, Cecile added, "*Désolée, ma chérie*, I meant homely. And why on earth isn't he tempted to get into your—"

"Shh, Ceci. I've had quite enough," Hélène glared at her colleague, "of your speculations. Not only are you insulting me, by insinuating that Marc's cheating on me, but you're imagining I have the indecency to take on a lover."

From across the yard, two pigtails swung around. In a

squeaky voice, Therese queried, "*Vraiment*, Hélène? You mean you don't have a lover? But everyone in the office says—"

"Do us a favor, Therese. Go out and sell some cookies," yelled Cecile, flinging alfalfa sprouts in her direction.

❖

After popping her range-free chicken in the oven, Hélène smiled at Chaussette. "Think we have time for another fashion show, *bébé*?"

Chaussette meowed.

"*Super*, that's what I thought." Hélène raced up the stairs. One by one, she donned all her new outfits. Chaussette watched the show, bobbing her head to the background pop music.

All of the outfits were soft and sleek, with gentle colors, accentuating Hélène's new natural, carefree style and slimmer figure. Discreet earrings, light makeup, and a dash of lipstick were all she needed to feel feminine and sexy. She ran her fingers through her fresh, sleek haircut and smiled at herself. *This is true bliss. Why didn't I do this years ago?*

She slipped on the last of her purchases: a tight, low-cut raspberry top, with fitted black pants. Chaussette watched with wide eyes as her mistress transformed herself into a *femme fatale*. Hélène blushed at the seductive woman staring at her in the mirror. Her hormones were racing as she dabbed French perfume between her breasts. Feeling their tips harden, her eyes lingered on the two buttons poking out of her thin cotton top.

I can't resist. Cupping her breasts, she blew kisses to herself in the mirror. "*Ouais, ouais*," she purred, drawing full circles with her boobs. She drew a few circles clockwise, then counterclockwise. "*Ouais, ouais*, I feel so sexy..."

Just then, a naughty grin spread over Hélène's face. Ever so slowly, her fingers gravitated south. Just as she unfastened her belt buckle, the front door slammed.

Hélène gasped, fixed her belt, and snatched a tissue. But she could only rub off half her lipstick. She rubbed harder. *Mince, it won't come off.*

Oh well. She started ripping off her sexy top. Then she remembered her talk with Cecile. Adrenaline spread through her body. *Je m'en fous. The heck with it!*

Sticking her fingers under the faucet, she raked them through her hair.

"Home already, *chéri?*" she hollered, bounding down the stairs, cradling Chaussette in her arms like a baby.

❖

Sylvie stood in the dimness of her darkroom. Aside from the red light casting shadows around her, she could barely see her fingers. As usual, the chemicals floating in the cramped space made her head spin. She was hanging the last photo when her cell phone rang.

She reached for her backpack but stopped abruptly. *Non! You've got to get Lydia out of your mind and out of your system. She's no good for you.*

To distract her thoughts, she peered through the darkness at the dozen glistening photos of Goldie hanging before her. As she was wiping her hands on her jeans, she felt a lump in one of her pockets. She pulled out a crumpled piece of paper.

Squinting in the dim, reddish light, she saw a phone number written on it.

Grabbing her backpack, she left the darkroom, shielding her eyes from the piercing light of the outside world.

❖

Hélène sashayed into the kitchen and dropped her precious kitty. Chaussette darted to her dish to gobble her kibble. "Go on, *ma petite*. Attack time!" Hélène had always relished those familiar crunching noises. She leaned against the counter, trying to appear relaxed.

Marc unceremoniously entered, dumping his stuff on the floor. He cast a glance at Hélène, smoothing imaginary wrinkles from her trousers.

His eyes narrowed. "What's up?"

"Ah, nothing. Just some new clothes I bought on sale." She performed a pirouette. "What do you think?"

Marc twisted the tip of his mustache.

Hélène took a step back. *I hate it when he twists that stupid thing. Wish he'd just shave it off.*

"Go ahead and waste your money." Marc glanced at the oven, pinching his nose. "And what's that awful burning smell?"

"*Mince*, the chicken!" When Hélène opened the oven, black smoke filled the kitchen.

"*Mon Dieu*, every time I come home, I get another great surprise. *Bravo*, Hélène. You hit the jackpot tonight!" Marc groped his way out of the smoky kitchen.

After an interminably long meal of half-burnt chicken, Hélène stood at the sink, contemplating a dirty dish in her hands. She watched the yellow grease slide off.

Beurk. Her hand went to her aproned belly to calm her nauseous feelings.

Chaussette, curled comfortably on a kitchen chair, meowed at her mistress.

"At least Maman never burns your dinners, *n'est-ce pas, bébé?*"

The cat yawned.

"I thought he'd at least say *something* about my new clothes. Maybe Cecile's right. I'm just too naïve." Hélène sighed. "Anyway, who cares? I bought them for me." She touched Chaussette's nose with a soapy finger. "And you, *bien sûr.*"

Just then, Marc entered and grabbed a beer from the fridge. When he popped off the cap, Chaussette pounced on it.

"I'll tell you what I think," he announced, taking a big, sudsy swig. "I can't stand your new look." He stared long and hard at Hélène's tight, black pants. "You're way more attractive in those long skirts of yours."

Marc began pacing. Shaking his head between generous sips of beer, he broke into a rough, home-spun song: "Twenty years ago I married a woman named Hélène Dupont. Basically, a shy, pleasant, and kind person. Nothing extraordinary, just pleasant, kind, and rather quiet. The kind of wife all men want. Don't they? Then she faints at work and falls off her chair. And what in the heck happens? Overnight, this woman becomes a total stranger in my household. *C'est incroyable.* She wakes up and turns into—"

Hélène couldn't suppress the amusement on her face, so Marc raised his voice: "A granola-eating, feminist jock." He ended his speech with a bang as he slammed his beer bottle on the kitchen table.

Hélène and Chaussette, both at the table, jumped up at the same time.

"Aaaiiee!" yelped Hélène. "Isn't he ridiculous, *bébé?*"

Hélène looked disbelievingly at her husband. Somehow, his face had transformed. Even with the mustache, it resembled a little boy's more than a grown man's. She held her breath when he took a swig of beer and began reciting another poem:

"My wife, Hélène, only eats greens, despises caffeine, gets up at dawn to stick her derrière in the *piscine*—God only knows why—and dresses like a drag queen. Just to please herself and her retarded cat." Ever so proudly, he flashed a mouthful of teeth at his wife and her pet.

Hélène snorted with laughter, while her black-and-white cat scurried out of the kitchen in horror. "I'm impressed. You've got real talent!" burst Hélène. "Maybe I should start drawing, since it's evident that you're the one who should be writing poems around here." She gave a final snort for emphasis. But her smile soon faded.

❖

Sylvie opened the crumpled piece of paper. The phone number was written in a purple felt pen and underneath, there was a small heart next to the name: *Nadine*. After that, it said: *Call me.*

Sylvie fingered the paper, pondering what to do. *If she's still in school, she can't be older than twenty-three. I'm way too old for this kind of game.* She crumpled the paper into a ball and aimed for the trash can.

Then she stopped. *But she* was *cute. And that gorgeous figure, in those jeans, and...Non. I can't.* She ripped the paper into ant-sized shreds.

There's no way I can piece these together, she reassured herself, flinging the bits into the trash can.

"There's got to be someone else out there. *N'est-ce pas*, Goldilocks?"

The orange cat looked up from her kibble and meowed in consensus.

❖

Later that evening, Hélène found her kitty huddled under the kitchen table. When she crouched down, Chaussette licked her mistress's chin. The rough little tongue tickled like mad, but Hélène was hardly in the mood to laugh.

"What do I do now, *bébé*? He says he doesn't know me anymore. But *I* don't even know me anymore. All I know is I'm messing up my marriage. And I have no idea why. Things were better before, weren't they, *ma puce*?" A fat tear trickled down Hélène's cheek.

As she sniveled on her kitty's fur, she noticed Marc's things lying on the linoleum.

When will he ever grow up?

Standing, she tossed his suit jacket over a chair.

A moment later, her eyes ventured back to Marc's jacket. *Guess it can't hurt to check.*

She sniffed at the starched collar. *Beurk!* She wrinkled her nose at the manly, sour odor. *This is going straight to the cleaners.*

Then a short black hair caught her eye. She plucked the hair from the collar; her fingers trembled as she inspected it. "*Whose* is this?" She gulped.

Chaussette rubbed against her mistress's ankles, meowing.

"Not now, *bébé*. Maman is trying to figure out—"

"Meow," insisted the cat.

Hélène flashed her an annoyed look. "I'll pet you as soon as—"

"Meow, meow," insisted the cat, even louder.

Hélène bent down. "What is it, *bébé*?"

She peered at her cat. Then she looked at the short, black hair in her hand.

Then her eyes went back to the kitty. *"Mon Dieu, bébé,* I'm such an idiot!" she whispered, draping her arms over Chaussette.

"Voilà." She stuck the black hair into her cat's furry neck. "Maybe it'll grow back if I plant it just right." She bit her lip as a tear of relief tumbled down her cheek.

Hélène tiptoed back to Marc's jacket. Hesitating, she weighed the pros and cons of her actions. *What would Cecile do?* After a millisecond, she knew. *Of course she would,* she decided, sliding her fingers into the inner pocket of his jacket.

Hmm…Wonder what this is? she asked herself, holding up a few neatly folded pages.

She glanced at the kitchen door. The noise from the living room was reassuring: screaming soccer fans. *He won't be in here for a while…unless he runs out of beer.*

She unfolded the pages, revealing sketches of racing cars and engines, except for the last one—a detailed drawing of a man's torso.

"What the heck is this?" she uttered under her breath as she inspected the drawing. Wiry muscles, thin shoulders, scant chest hair. *When did he start sketching himself?*

Hélène's heart was racing. *And naked, of all things!*

A disturbing thought popped into her head. *Who is this for?*

Her shoulders sagged. Evidently, it wasn't for her. Otherwise, he would've given it to her, instead of stashing it in his pocket. This brought up another unsettling question. When was the last time she saw him naked?

She remembered the spring weekend they had spent together in Namur, for a distant cousin's wedding. *Non. The walls were too thin, and the bed was miniscule.*

Her mind reeled further back, to the summer at Ostende

beach. *Oui, that's it. Nearly two years ago.* Her heart sank at the thought.

Just then, the soccer fans quieted down. Hélène glanced at the door, quickly folded the sketches, and shoved them into Marc's breast pocket. All but the torso sketch, which she stuffed in her apron pocket before cranking up the radio. The melodious songs helped tune out the nagging question: *Who is this for?*

Even Chaussette couldn't help with this one.

After a while, Hélène slumped into a chair with her new recipe book. As she pondered innovative vegetarian dishes, her mind kept returning to the notebook.

She had a beast of a time keeping her paws out of her apron pocket.

CHAPTER FOURTEEN

D r. Duprès took Hélène's hand. The warm touch of the doctor's fingers had a pacifying effect.

"You've come so far. *Franchement*, I'm impressed. You must continue with the dieting and exercise." The older woman gazed into her patient's azure eyes. "I'm sorry to learn your husband isn't supporting you in this."

"He bought me a bike. That's about it."

"*C'est étrange*. You'd think he'd be proud of your efforts. You look younger and more confident."

"That's what he hates the most."

"That you seem younger?"

"*Non*. More confident."

"Maybe he's the jealous type?"

"Marc? *Jaloux?*" Hélène snickered. "That would be the day. He hardly looks at me."

Dr. Duprès raised an eyebrow. "But you said he doesn't like your new look."

"He only notices what he doesn't like; he's always been like that—he's always on the defensive as if everyone were out to get him." Hélène took a deep breath. "But don't get me wrong, *Docteur*. So far, he's never even cared enough to be jealous. Besides, there's absolutely no reason—"

Just then, a young nurse knocked on the door to request Dr. Duprès's assistance.

The doctor rose. "Sorry, Hélène. Will you excuse me for a moment?"

She left her alone, to reflect on their conversation. That's when Hélène started to notice a bitter taste in her mouth.

As Hélène waited for the doctor to return, her thoughts were racing. *There's absolutely no reason why he would be jealous because...* Then, abruptly, Hélène's mind shut down. Everything grew fuzzy in the small office. The medical files swelled as if they were alive.

Turning toward the window, Hélène spotted two yellow and gray dots on a branch. She squinted until the dots sprouted into two tiny birds, pecking at each other's feathers with pointy beaks. They stopped pecking. One started stroking the other.

She strained her ears to hear their baby chirps through the glass. But instead of chirps, she heard gurgling sounds near her belly. Her hand went to massage her stomach, until she spotted the fish tank. Tiny bubbles were popping up to the surface, making the gurgling noise in the tank.

Giggling at her mistake, Hélène watched the pair of goldfish swimming around each other. One was hovering behind a clump of seaweed, hiding. The plumper one kept darting behind the seaweed to chase the other.

Hélène leaned against the wall and shut her eyes while her imagination took over her senses.

The two women are bathing in the ocean, off the Belgian coast. They are holding hands and laughing as they jump against the waves. All of a sudden, a massive swell hits them, and Hélène loses hold of Sylvie's hand. After the wave crashes, Sylvie makes her way to the surface. When Hélène doesn't reappear, Sylvie dives under to search for her.

After several minutes, she finally brings Hélène, unconscious, to the surface. Although Sylvie is struggling to catch her breath, she places her ear over Hélène's mouth to see if she is breathing. She isn't. She pries open her mouth to make sure there are no obstructions—no seaweed preventing her from breathing freely. The air passage is clear. Next, she grips her tightly and flips her over. Seawater streams out of Hélène's mouth. Once her lungs are empty, Sylvie sweeps her up and runs to shore. Kneeling next to her unconscious student, she listens again for air. Then she seals her mouth over Hélène's cool lips.

Just when Hélène feels Sylvie's warm lips over her own, and her strong hands on her chest, she hears a distant "ahem."

Hélène opened her eyes, but instead of a sexy lifeguard rousing her, she saw a familiar pair of sturdy shoes under a white lab coat.

"Therapeutic, *n'est-ce pas?*"

"Excuse me?" Hélène stared blankly at Dr. Duprès.

"The bubble sounds."

Hélène turned her attention to the goldfish tank. The fish were nibbling at each other. "I wonder what it's like to live underwater." She scrunched her nose to the glass. *The bigger one's seducing the little one.* "Must be heavenly," she added, closing her eyelids halfway as her thoughts returned to her daydream.

"It's the newest in air filters. Hi-tech—straight from Japan."

Hélène lifted an eyebrow.

"But we're not here to chat about fish, are we?" inquired Dr. Duprès, limping toward her. "It might sound strange to you, but perhaps you should consider that some men are just like that. You know, different than women."

She's right about that one, thought Hélène, remembering Sylvie's lips on hers. Even though she had only imagined this for a split second, they seemed so real. So soft. *Marc's lips never feel like anything, except prickly. All because of that stupid mustache he's always trimming and tweaking, like some sort of bonsai bush.*

Hélène had never liked mustaches, and in all these years, she hadn't revealed this to her husband, who was so proud of his.

The doctor's voice droned on. "They don't always understand our feelings, our emotions...and they can be so stubborn. It might just take some time for your husband to come around. The newness needs to wear off first." Dr. Duprès placed her hand on Hélène's shoulder. "You know, husbands protest, but after a while, they always give in. So don't worry. He'll get used to the new you. And in no time, he'll be treating you like a princess."

"Let's be realistic, *Docteur*." Hélène grimaced. "You've already met Marc. I can't imagine him loving my new look. Or even accepting it, for that matter."

Dr. Duprès glanced at her watch. "I'm sorry, Hélène, but our time is up. I'd like you to get a blood test tomorrow on an empty stomach. We'll have the results in a few days." She pulled out a form, checked off the items to be analyzed, and handed it to her.

As Hélène exited the hospital, she inserted her fingernail into her mouth.

She was about to chew but stopped. *What are you doing? You gave this up on your wedding night. It grosses Marc out, remember?* She pulled her finger out of her mouth.

Then a naughty look swept over her face. *It's never too late to change your mind.*

Ever so gleefully, Hélène chomped on her first nail in two decades.

❖

After another disastrous, unromantic evening, the couple learned their lesson. For the rest of the week, Marc stayed downstairs to flip channels on the tube, while Hélène scrubbed dishes and escaped with Chaussette to work on her poems in the bedroom.

On Thursday night, Hélène sat in her nightgown, squinting at the words she had just typed on the screen. The room was pitch dark except for a string of light from the mini lamp clamped to her desk. Chaussette's head bobbed at her mistress's illuminated knuckles as they rose and fell over the keyboard.

All of a sudden, the words appeared fuzzy. Hélène tapped the keys a few more times and peered at the screen again. She could barely make out the sentence: *A vivid sunburst from the horizon...*

She scowled at the dictionaries strewn over her desk and piled around her fluffy slippers. Her mind was focused on Marc rather than her writing. Tonight, instead of rugby, football, or wrestling, BBC News was blaring downstairs. Each time she tried to tune out the newscaster's forceful voice, it grew louder.

She glanced at her watch. *Already ten. So he wants to learn English. Fine. But why now?*

After a pensive minute, Hélène forced herself to resume typing. To her delight, her thoughts tumbled onto the keyboard, fashioning the lushest scenes she'd ever imagined. The deeper she let her mind go, the more seeds her imagination sowed.

Finally, it led her to a secluded green spot surrounded by the wildest forms of nature—just what she needed to revive her soul.

"Exotic, tropical trees, flowers, butterflies…A gorgeous mountain, bright blue sky, a marvelous pond," she whispered to Chaussette.

After working nonstop for thirty minutes, she felt drowsy. "I'll just shut my eyes for a minute," she mumbled, crossing her arms over the keyboard.

Instantly, Hélène's mind drew her into a world of homespun poetry bursting with adventure.

Her eyelids serve as the movie screen as her poem comes to life: tropical trees swaying in the breeze, exotic flowers beaming at the sun, butterflies flitting in the air. Hélène is standing next to Sylvie in a deep pond. Ducks and water lilies surround their naked bodies. Over Sylvie's bare shoulders looms a stunning mountain. Both women are smiling at each other. Hélène doesn't want to interrupt this peaceful moment, but the pair has been soaking in the water for over an hour, and her fingertips are soggy. She swims toward the grassy edge of the pond. As soon as she lifts her foot onto a rock, Sylvie places a firm hand on her shoulder.

"Attends…We're not done yet. I want you to swim a bit longer. I'd like to check your style again."

Slowly, Hélène turns around. Sylvie's eyes are glistening as much as her breasts, which are dripping with water, and just as luscious.

Hélène whispers, "You push me really hard, you know."

"But you like to be pushed, non?" teases Sylvie, whose voice is so raspy it sounds like it has gravel in it.

Her Greek accent is even sexier in the water, Hélène

realizes, feeling her cheeks sizzle. Before she can react, Sylvie yanks her off the rock, and she falls back into the water. Sylvie dives under the surface and swiftly retrieves her victim. To keep her buoyant, she pulls Hélène to her bare bosom, causing her student's nipples to arch toward the sky. Hélène's chest, safely nestled in her instructor's muscular arms, rapidly rises and falls.

"Super, you're still breathing," says Sylvie with a chuckle. Gradually, her student's body relaxes in her arms. Everything grows soft, except for Hélène's nipples, which are now as erect as tiny thimbles.

"Let's check to see if you're conscious," whispers Sylvie. With a sly grin, she draws a figure-eight in the air and exclaims "Aha!" as she pokes her student's nipple.

"Aaaiiee!" gasps Hélène, knocking the offending finger away.

Sylvie chuckles. "Just routine testing. Oui, the victim's still alive."

"Help!" Hélène yelps. "I've been rescued by the nastiest lifeguard in the pond."

She presses her bare body against her instructor's moist breasts. "Somebody save me!"

Sylvie laughs as she leans toward her victim's mouth, with her hand on her...

Firm fingers shook Hélène's shoulder.

"Ah, you're so bad..." murmured Hélène with pleasure.

"It's time for bed."

Hélène woke with a start. *Marc?* Her mind was still fuzzy. She shook her head.

The room was bright now. She rubbed her eyes and swiveled in her chair. Her husband was standing near her, bending down, inserting a skinny leg into his pajamas. It was him all right—she recognized his elastic underwear strap and the tiny hairs trapped underneath.

Reality sucks. Dragging her slippers along the carpet, she headed into the bathroom to throw some icy water on her hot cheeks.

Hélène gasped when she saw her reflection in the mirror. As always, those same blue eyes were staring back at her, but this time, something deep inside seemed altered. It was hard to tell if they were glistening with excitement—or just plain scared. *What now?* She splashed cold water on her face. Its coolness was soothing. Keeping her eyes shut, she focused on the pink light filtering through her eyelids—her portable movie screen.

To her surprise, the Greek goddess reappeared, teasing her in the pond. She doused her face with more icy water to cleanse the image lurking in her mind. When at last she lifted her soggy head, a sheet of wetness trickled from her chin. As it drenched her thin nightgown, she felt her nipples moisten, then grow hard. To her embarrassment, the tightness of her tender, intimate flesh trapped under wet cotton excited her.

Before she could stop it, Hélène's finger rose in the air as a strange grin spread over her face. The finger drew a figure-eight in the air.

To her surprise, Hélène heard herself exclaim "Aha!" before poking herself in the nipple.

"Aaaiiiee!" she yelped in pain.

A groggy voice erupted from the bedroom. "What's going on in there? Your brush caught a snarl again?"

She ignored her husband's snide remarks. Even though her nipple was smarting, her finger rose again to give it another poke. *Ah, non!* Hélène's other hand knocked the offending finger away. *This is just like in my dream*, she realized with horror. *What's wrong with me?*

To stop her thoughts from pondering the imponderable, she donned a fresh nightgown and slathered night cream over her face. The cool white cream entered her pores, temporarily soothing her nerves. Then she tiptoed to her side of the bed and slid under the soft covers.

For the first time in years, Hélène snuggled up to her husband. She pressed her forehead against his warm, bony back, hoping it could somehow shelter her from danger.

None of this was very convincing, so she went a step further. Pinching her lips together, she inhaled deeply. The familiar odors impregnating Marc's pajamas hardly aroused pleasant sensations—on the contrary. But she was relieved they didn't downright disgust her either.

He is my husband. His odors are my odors, and mine are his. Married couples are supposed to share odors and love each other anyway.

Hélène took another whiff and wrinkled her nose.

At least, that's how it's supposed to be, non?

In the dimly lit bedroom, she could just make out the broad outline of Marc's shoulders.

Okay. I'm still not convinced. Let's take it a bit further.

Lifting her index finger, she traced the nape of Marc's neck until she located the object of her former obsession—a smooth, sexy, rebellious curl.

This just might work.

As she touched the magic curl, she became a teenager again, obsessed with the puppy love of her past. For a full, glorious minute, she forgot she was a grown, married woman, desperately hoping to comprehend—more accurately, hoping to reject—something that had become so real and evident in her new life, it hurt too much to even imagine the consequences.

❖

The next morning, Hélène shivered while standing in the shallow end of the pool. After such a sleepless night, her body felt fragile as the coolness of the water penetrated her skin. Her thoughts, too, were muddled; throughout the lesson, she pursed her lips to force them away.

As an additional measure, she kept a safe distance from her instructor. *Hopefully, she'll just think I have my period.*

After a painful, soggy hour, Hélène removed her goggles and squinted at the clock.

Enfin, it's over. I can't wait to get out of here.

Wading past Sylvie, she began to climb out of the pool.

Until her teacher grasped her shoulder.

"*Attends*. We're not done yet. I want you to swim a bit longer." Sylvie's voice was husky. "Just one more lap, okay? I'd like to check your style again."

Hélène turned toward Sylvie. "You push me really hard, you know."

As soon as she said this, goose bumps erupted on her arms. *This is déjà-vu.* She hardly heard the raspy reply: "But you like to be pushed, *non*?"

When Sylvie flashed her a coy smile, Hélène cringed. Before her instructor could notice her flushed face, Hélène dove into the water and started swimming the crawl. She could feel the adrenaline pumping through her veins as she kicked fiercely. Her powerful strokes propelled her body over the surface, like a water bug. While she tore through the pool, her imagination soared:

Last night was a dream. But this is real. Do I really like it when she pushes me? That's a scary thought. What would Marc think? Anyway, who cares what he thinks? I certainly don't. Not anymore. I admire her. No, I don't. Yes, I do. Non, je...

When she reached the shallow end, she struck a fleshy blob in the water. Standing, she saw the Greek goddess's outstretched hand. She was laughing.

"*Incroyable!* I said one lap, not five!"

"Guess I got a bit carried away."

Sylvie waved her timer in front of her pupil's nose. "You sure did. *Super.* Congratulations, Hélène. You just passed the final test," she gushed, extending her hand.

Hélène gave her a puzzled look.

Without waiting, Sylvie pulled her into her arms and planted a kiss on each cheek.

What's going on? wondered Hélène, stiffening.

Sylvie's eyes were glistening. "I'm so proud of you, Hélène. You're amazing. You've only been coming here for a month, and you already swim like a pro."

"Let's not exaggerate." Hélène pulled away. "But thanks for the compliment."

"You deserve it," said Sylvie, hopping out of the water.

Hélène watched in awe as her instructor's strong legs stalked over to the bench, leaving a moist trail in their wake. Wrapping her magnificent body in a bath towel, she lowered herself to the pool's edge. With her toes dangling in the water, she tapped the space next to her.

"Come over here for a sec."

Hélène's knees quivered underwater. Deep down, she knew Sylvie had something in store for her—something she never, ever would have imagined.

Enveloped in a towel covering as much flesh as possible, Hélène managed a few awkward tiptoes toward the poolside. She tried to settle—more elegantly than *elephantly*—next to the stunning Greek presence. She held her breath as she dipped her pale toes into the chilly water.

After a pause, Sylvie spoke. "I've really enjoyed teaching you, Hélène."

"I'm enjoying our lessons too," responded Hélène, staring at the other end of the pool.

"Actually, Friday will be our last lesson together."

The words didn't sink in right away. Hélène turned brusquely toward her. "What did you say?"

Sylvie spoke gently, which further emphasized her Greek accent. "Friday will be our last lesson. Now that you—"

Hélène gasped. "*Quoi?* Our last lesson? What do you mean? I thought—"

"You're a perfect swimmer now, Hélène. You just proved it." She patted Hélène's knee. "You don't need my help anymore."

"But that's only the crawl!" stammered Hélène, ignoring the tingle rising up her thigh. "There's still the breaststroke, the backstroke, and that other one. The..." she stammered. "The...the..."

"Butterfly."

Hélène's throat went dry. "*Oui*, the butterfly," she croaked.

A hint of confusion flashed over Sylvie's face. She opened her mouth, but Hélène beat her to it.

"I've still got tons to learn, and I want you to teach me all the strokes!" she insisted, grabbing Sylvie's muscular arm. She realized her face was turning scarlet, but she didn't care.

"I didn't expect this at all." Sylvie shook her head. "The director told me you had a budget."

"*Non!* I need those other strokes. We have to do them all. I want to swim like you, Sylvie. So you have to keep teaching me." *I want to be like you, Sylvie,* said a little voice in Hélène's head, right before an onslaught of emotions hit her, like knives slicing through her heart. She lowered her flustered face. Despite the blood racing through her veins, she saw her toes were turning blue. *So what? Go ahead, turn blue. And drop off, for all I care,* she ordered them, suppressing her urge to kick at the water like a mad dog.

The wet women shifted uncomfortably as they sat beside each other on the cold cement. For a few painfully silent seconds, the timer dangling from Sylvie's neck ticked so loudly, Hélène was tempted to rip it off her neck.

Do something! Say something! her mind pleaded.

But Sylvie simply stared at the other side of the pool.

At last, she turned to Hélène. "I don't know what to say. If I'd only known." She swallowed slowly. "I hate to say this, but I just accepted another job on the other side of Brussels. I start next Monday."

"*Quoi?*" Hélène looked stunned, as if someone had just smacked her skull. "You mean you won't be teaching here anymore? Ever again?"

❖

Sylvie brushed a wet strand of hair out of Hélène's eyes. She felt a pinch in her heart when she looked at those sad blue eyes, which were as moist as her student's hair. Averting her gaze, she confirmed, "I'm sorry, Hélène. Our lessons are over."

Choking back tears, Hélène jumped up and—trailing her towel behind her in nearsighted confusion—scrambled away like an injured bee.

"*Attention!*" Sylvie yelled. But her warning came too late.

"Aaaiiee!" Hélène cursed as her face smacked into

the Poolside Rules sign. Without stopping, she ran around the sign—vibrating with a "Doooiiing...Doooiiing"—and vanished from Sylvie's view.

"Rule number one: no running," whispered Sylvie as her moist, dark eyes followed a trail of chaotic footprints into the locker room.

❖

There was that old pain again—raw, incessant. Like when she fell down and skinned her knee as a kid. Hélène wished she could just weep away the agonizing sensations taking over her body. *But you can't. You're an adult now*, she told herself, peering at her throbbing nose in the mirror. *Hope it doesn't swell. Why do I have to be so darn nearsighted?*

She threw her glasses onto the counter. They slammed against the wall.

More destructive thoughts invaded Hélène's mind as she sat on her locker room stool, struggling to dry her tangles.

I can't stand even being here, she realized, avoiding her blurry image in the mirror. *Je déteste...*

The hair dryer was so loud, she didn't hear the water stop running in the shower. Nor did she hear the soft rubber sounds of thongs pattering across the tile floor.

A figure approached her from behind. Startled, Hélène reached for her glasses.

Sure enough, Sylvie stood behind her with a towel loosely wrapped around her slim figure. The white terry cloth brought out the silkiness of her dark skin. Hélène shivered.

She really is a Greek goddess. Elégante...sensuelle.

She shivered even more when Sylvie placed her hot fingers on her shoulders.

Hélène shut off the hair dryer.

The two women gazed at each other in the misty mirror. Neither said a word.

Hélène felt a twitch in her spine. She shifted her weight to smother it—anything to distract her mind from the mounting tension in the steamy locker room.

At last, Sylvie broke the silence. "I feel so bad leaving you like this. I had no idea you wanted more, Hélène."

You had no idea I wanted more? Hélène felt a lump rising in her throat. *Well, neither did I. Or did I?* "I learned more than swimming with you. I caught your enthusiasm for..." Hélène's throat choked; before she could stop herself, she uttered: "Life."

Sylvie chuckled. "Don't be silly."

Hélène replied gravely, "*Non*, really. You taught me to try to be the best I could be. And accept who I am."

Sylvie squeezed her student's shoulder. "You deserve it."

Hélène knew she was blushing, especially with Sylvie's fingers digging into her flesh. She forced herself to continue. "I've always considered what people would think before I did something. I was hardly living—until now."

Sylvie shook her gently by the shoulders. "You did it yourself. I just showed you the way."

The corners of Hélène's mouth rose as Sylvie lightly rocked her.

"It really means a lot to me," whispered Hélène, gripping the counter in case her enthusiasm—and Sylvie's lingering touch—propelled her off her stool. She resisted the temptation to drop her head, to conceal the heat invading her cheeks.

Sylvie smiled broadly. "*Ca alors.* I wish all my students were as appreciative as you."

"You're a great teacher." Hélène gulped back the lump rising in her throat. "I really wish I could continue. I'd like to learn the other strokes."

"I wish you could too, but that's impossible." Sylvie gave her shoulders one last squeeze. Raking her fingers through her dark, glistening hair, she whispered, "I'm so sorry," flinging little droplets into the air.

Me too, believe me. Hélène shuddered as the cool drops soaked through her blouse. *At least I get a souvenir from the pool.*

❖

Hélène was about to turn her hair dryer back on when Sylvie's eyes lit up. "*Attends*, I've got an idea!"

"*Quoi?*" asked Hélène, trying to conceal her emotions.

"The pool opens at eight on Saturday mornings, so why don't we ask if I can reserve a lane for us before all the kids show up?"

Hélène burst out, "That's a great idea!" Her eyes met Sylvie's. *I knew this would work out.* She resisted the temptation to lick her lips. *The energy between us is too strong for something stupid like a scheduling problem to...*

Then Hélène's face fell.

Sylvie leaned forward. "What's wrong?"

Hélène sighed heavily. "I forgot. Marc and I go to the market on Saturday mornings."

"So go later."

"I can't. He likes to go early, to beat the crowds."

Sylvie crossed her muscular arms. "So let him beat the crowds by himself. He's a big boy."

Hélène considered the idea. Then she frowned. "*Non.* He'd rip my arm off if I didn't come along."

Sylvie's smile melted. "He would?" she asked gravely, staring into Hélène's deep blue eyes.

Their bodies were so close, Hélène could feel her teacher's

breath on her face. Her heart fluttered. *"Mais non!* Don't be silly," she stammered, leaning back.

"You never know. I saw how he..." Sylvie paused. "Anyway, we'd be done by nine. He could come pick you up on the way."

"Wait. Marc...Here?" Hélène shuddered at the thought of him at the pool: staring at them in the water, peeking into the locker room, waiting impatiently for her to shower. *What a nightmare!* But she desperately wanted to continue their lessons.

She took a deep breath. "Can I think about it?"

Sylvie swept her fingers through her hair, dousing Hélène with more souvenirs from the pool. "Of course. Just tell me tomorrow."

Hélène exhaled with relief. *"Merci, Sylvie."* Impulsively, she touched her teacher's arm and—for the very first time in her life—winked at a woman.

Chapter Fifteen

Hélène was still practicing her winking technique as she parked her bike in front of the office. In the ladies' room, she wiped the sweat off her face, and—like an excited racehorse—began pacing in front of the stalls. Hot air left her nostrils at the beat of her thumping heart.

Ducking under the metallic doors, she scanned for signs of shoes.

"*Super!*" she exclaimed, righting herself. "Nobody's here."

Despite her matted helmet hair and sweaty clothes, she felt fabulous.

She approached the mirror to inspect the healthy glow radiating from her face. It beamed back at her. She winked. It winked back. She leaned forward. The face approached hers.

Clear eyes, turquoise like the sea...

She wiggled her body, relishing how free it roamed under her sports clothes, enjoying the pleasure of Lycra flirting with her moist skin. She felt the power of her thigh muscles as she gyrated her hips.

"You've been working out for nearly two hours, with no complaints. And it's not even nine in the morning." She gave herself a seductive wink before disappearing into a stall. "You've come a long way, *bébé*!"

Hélène's confidence soon faded, however. After two painful hours at the computer, she went straight to the kitchen and fixed herself a double espresso to relieve her throbbing head.

I shouldn't do this, but... she thought as she loaded her mug with milk and six spoonfuls of sugar. Then she cocked her head and drained the mug. And before the caffeine reached her system, she slugged back another double.

Just then, Cecile entered the kitchen. Her dainty nose sniffed the coffee smell in the air. She squinted her eyes at Hélène. "Aren't you supposed to be avoiding caffeine?"

"It's just so hard to be good all the time, Ceci." Hélène chuckled nervously. Her ears began to tingle, which always happened when she felt guilty. "I'm sick of watching what I eat all the time. People take vacations, so why can't our bodies take vacations too?"

Cecile's lips broke into a grin. "*Tout à fait.* That's what I've been trying to tell you, *ma puce.*" She clinked her mug with Hélène's. "Stop being such a goody-goody and do something outrageous. I dare you."

Cecile gave her a wink and sauntered out of the kitchen.

Hélène was still smirking at Cecile's remark as she poked her head into the fridge. Way in the back, she unearthed an old package of cookies. Ignoring the expiration date, she gobbled down—like a farm hog—the entire package of sweet, crunchy cookies.

Powdery crumbs tumbled from her lips onto her blouse, but Hélène didn't care; she was on a roll. Pulling a half gallon of chocolate milk from the fridge, she guzzled the syrupy stuff directly from the carton. With chocolate bubbles dribbling from the corners of her mouth, she crumpled the empty container and, like a pro basketball star, launched it over her shoulder.

"*Ouais, deux points!*" she exclaimed when it ricocheted into the trash.

Hélène reentered her office giddy and out of breath. Ignoring bits of soggy chocolate tumbling from her mouth, she plopped in her chair and, with a judicious tongue swipe, licked the last bit of evidence off her lips.

"*Merveilleux!*" she declared, winking at her plants— innocent accomplices in her hedonistic crime. But shortly afterward, she felt the disastrous effects of her gluttony: translating with one hand while rubbing her stomach with the other, mind buzzing, stomach bursting.

Losing control in the kitchen was not such a brilliant idea after all.

Stuffing the Santorini painting into her bag, Hélène forced herself to breathe steadily as she inched her way down the hall. Playing hooky was outrageous, wasn't it? She'd never even taken a sick day before. As she tiptoed past her boss's office, she vowed to make Ceci proud.

❖

Hélène felt instantly lighter as soon as she left the office. The cool air filled her lungs with freshness as tufts of hair blew around her face, caressing her softly in the breeze. Despite this temporary relief from pain, she couldn't wait to get home and collapse. However, as soon as she pedaled down a familiar street lined with shops, she saw her optometrist standing in his window. She squeezed hard on the brakes, just in time to see him hold up a pair of glasses.

Hélène forgot all about her stomach pains and entered the shop. A few minutes later, she was beaming as she biked away. Her stylish new glasses accentuated her features, and with much thinner lenses, she felt lighter and more carefree.

She pedaled to a red light. *Hmm, what should I do now?* A devilish look swept across her face. When it turned green, she made a sharp right toward the pool.

It's time I tell her what's on my mind.

Hélène pedaled feverishly. Once she reached the familiar building, she threw her bike on the grass. As she raced up the concrete steps, four giggling teenage girls were just leaving. Hélène tried to get out of their way—but it was too late. Her momentum propelled her forward. She lurched to the right to avoid the girls and tripped on the steps.

"*Mince!*" she cried, toppling backward.

The girls stood staring at the blond woman lying unceremoniously on the steps.

"Are you all right, *Madame*?" one of them asked, giggling.

Hélène dusted off her behind. *Runts*, she sighed, clutching her new glasses to her chest. She felt suddenly fragile as if the girls had just sucked every last ounce of confidence from her—confidence that had taken weeks to build.

Like a fragile bird, she stood at the top of the steps, only meters from the pool. Instead of opening the door, she hesitated. Dark clouds loomed overhead; goose bumps erupted on her forearms as a chill swept through her body. Time stopped during this moment of indecision.

Just when she decided to enter the building, a beam of light hit her from behind. She spun around. Some mysterious force was radiating incredibly warm, soothing energy. She could feel it penetrating not only her skin, melting her goose bumps, but her entire soul.

This is amazing. The light seemed to be emanating from the parking lot. Squinting, she searched for its source. She looked up to see a sliver between the dark clouds.

Hélène shielded her eyes from the piercing light.

Spontaneously, she spread her arms and opened her heart to the penetrating light. *Whoever you are, or whatever you are, guide me. I'm ready.*

She stood immobilized like a statue on top of the steps, eyes closed and palms up, for a full minute. The warm sunlight licked her face as she basked in its vitalizing force. Breathing deeply, she offered her body, mind, and soul to this illuminating source of energy, surrendering to its touch. She realized her entire being was craving an answer, even though she hadn't yet formulated her question.

Hélène's reply appeared when the clouds shifted. The penetrating light dimmed, revealing its true source: light reflected off a car door mirror, hitting her directly in the face.

Squinting, she realized that the car was an old yellow VW bug.

That's when she knew the answer. *Life can be so easy. But why am I always doubting myself?*

Instead of entering the pool building, she plopped on the grass beside her bike and a rusty trash can. Crossing her legs, she let her face drop into her hands, like a wilted flower, breathing steadily with her eyes shut. Her auditory and olfactory senses intensified.

Something smells bizarre.

Hélène sniffed her fingers. Then she chuckled.

Trash mixed with freshly cut grass, mixed with cookies and syrupy espresso...What a bizarre day. And it's not even noon.

She glanced at the pool building, then at the thunderclouds looming overhead.

I must really be a poet. Or else I'm completely bonkers.

❖

Hélène checked her watch again. *12:25 p.m. already. Doesn't she ever take a break?*

Ignoring her rumbling belly, she turned her attention back to her notebook. The blue ink was splotchy in some spots, and the letters were terribly slanted, forcing her sentences downward.

It's the strangest day...

She continued with her entry, gripping her pen tightly as she released the words polluting her brain. The ink spilled onto the notebook's worn pages:

She must get rid of this overwhelming turmoil. Without even thinking, she lays down her deepest, hidden thoughts. She nearly bores holes through the paper, she's pressing so hard with her pen. She attacks her notebook with vengeance; she's never felt like this before. She's fully submerged with

Then something warm touched Hélène's shoulder. Jerking her head, she peered over her glasses. Although the person was out of focus, Hélène knew it was Sylvie. The warm tingle in her shoulder told her so. Adjusting her glasses, she squinted at the bright yellow raincoat looming above her.

Sylvie sported a friendly smile. "*Quelle bonne surprise.*" She squeezed Hélène's shoulder, then peered at her quizzically. "Aren't you working this afternoon?"

Hélène swiftly shut her notebook. "Well..."

She got up slowly, avoiding Sylvie's inquisitive eyes as she shook the grass off her pants. "*Oui.*" She licked her lips. "*Non.* Actually, I took the afternoon off."

Sylvie pointed to the bike sprawled on the grass. "So you went for a ride to the pool and..." Her eyes narrowed in on the notebook Hélène was clutching. "And what have we got here?"

Hélène swiveled her head toward a distant tree. "I needed some fresh air and—"

"Poetry, perhaps?"

Hélène's hands grew clammy. "It's...such a nice day," she stammered.

Looking up, Sylvie sniffed at the impending rain. The purple-black clouds appeared to be throbbing, like a day-old bruise. "Such a nice day," she scoffed. "For a soggy ride."

Sylvie nudged her. "I'm done for the day. Join me for lunch?"

Hélène snuck a glimpse at Sylvie's dark, glistening eyes. *One little meal can't hurt, non?*

"I'd love to."

With that response, Hélène's stomach gurgled loudly—a fresh souvenir of her cookie orgy in the kitchen—but it was too late. She was already struggling to keep up with the Greek athlete's long strides across the parking lot.

For every step Sylvie took, Hélène took two.

As she shuffled her boots on the damp asphalt, Hélène tried to figure out how to wipe the goofy smile off her face before Sylvie could see it.

"Promise you won't laugh?" Sylvie grinned, pulling out her keys.

Hélène nodded. But when Sylvie stopped before an old, yellow VW bug, Hélène's eyes bugged.

"Is this...Is this your car?"

"*M'enfin*, you said you wouldn't laugh."

"I'm not laughing, I swear. It's just that—"

"She's old. From the early eighties, but I don't care. She's family." Sylvie caressed the battered door of her banana-colored car. "And she runs just fine. You'll see." She yanked on the door three times. "Guess I'm lucky it hasn't fallen off its hinges."

At last, the door opened.

"Wait a sec." Sylvie dove inside to clear off the passenger's seat, and tossed a variety of items—CDs, various papers, a book of poems, a coupon for take-out pizza, a squash ball, and two rolls of film—onto the backseat.

"All's clear," she announced, flinging her raincoat on top of the pile and opening the passenger door.

Hélène entered the vehicle cautiously. As she sank into the tattered checkered seat, she tried to avoid thoughts of sunbaked chewing gum and other sticky substances.

Wonder what her house looks like? she speculated, tucking her hands safely in her lap.

Sylvie's eyes were twinkling. "Promise you won't laugh?"

"You already asked me that," replied Hélène, stiffening.

"Do you promise or not?"

"Sure, I promise."

"*D'accord.* Time to go fishing," announced Sylvie, bending over and thrusting her fingers under the driver's seat. At last, her head popped up.

She waved a yellow screwdriver before Hélène's eyes. "*Voilà!*"

She's weirder than I am. The thought made Hélène chuckle.

The swimming instructor inserted the tip of the screwdriver into the ignition.

"*Voilà!*" she repeated, flicking her wrist.

"*Mon Dieu!*" exclaimed Hélène as the engine revved up.

Sylvie flashed a coy smile. "I lost the key a couple of years ago."

"I see." Hélène bit her lip. *Boy, her teeth are white.*

"But don't tell anyone."

"They wouldn't believe me anyway," stated Hélène with a chuckle, before her face grew serious.

❖

As Sylvie concentrated on the road, Hélène's thoughts flipped back to the day they first met.

"So you really didn't need your keys to drive home that day at the market."

Sylvie shook her head. "All I care about is the keychain."

Hélène frowned at the passing trees, which seemed to be jeering at her as they flew past the window.

After an uncomfortably silent moment, she stole a glance at the Greek goddess, skillfully steering through the dense lunch-hour traffic. Instantly, all negative thoughts left Hélène's mind; she was too preoccupied with Sylvie's forearms as she firmly gripped the steering wheel. She felt a burst of pleasure as her teacher's arm muscles popped out with each swift maneuver. She even admired the tiny veins traveling over them, like little green canals.

Ever so discreetly, she let her eyes wander up Sylvie's arm.

Her biceps are so round and smooth, so well defined.

Hélène wrapped her fingers around her own bicep and gave it a squeeze; its insignificance made her cringe.

The best part was when Sylvie shifted gears. *This is intense.*

Hélène's eyes lingered over her instructor's strong fingers, and their power, as they gripped the stick propped between their bodies; the smooth control they offered excited Hélène.

She drives just like she swims, skillful and fast.

When they passed a bus, Hélène barely caught the blur of passengers' faces before the VW banana bug left it in the dust.

Her eyes sparkled as they drifted back to Sylvie's muscular forearms.

Wonder if she's as skillful and fast at everything she does?

The thought made her hair rise at the nape of her neck; she rolled down her window for a burst of air to douse the curious tingle spreading over her body.

❖

After maneuvering past a police car, Sylvie hollered into the wind. "Sorry my car's such a mess." She wrinkled her nose. "I meant to throw out that banana peel. I really did, but…"

She switched on the radio. Crackling Greek music blared out of the speakers.

"It's old, but it still works." Winking at Hélène, she fiddled with the dial until the crackling stopped.

The upbeat foreign music swept into Hélène's ears, transporting her to places she had never imagined, until Sylvie stopped at a red light.

"Hope you don't mind Greek food."

"Greek food?" Hélène gulped. *What in the heck does Greek food taste like?* She forced a smile. "Lovely. Great idea."

"Glad you like it." Sylvie swept a strand of hair behind her ear. "Cause that's all I ever eat." She gazed at her passenger, who was staring straight ahead. "What about you? Where do you usually go?"

"Go?"

"To eat."

"I don't know." Hélène pondered her options. "Actually, I don't."

Sylvie stared at her with disbelief. "You've got to be kidding. You don't go out?"

Hélène lowered her chin. "Not really. Not to eat, anyway."

"But that's insane!"

"Really?" Hélène began tracing circles on the side mirror. "Guess I never thought about it."

Sylvie turned down the Greek music. "I can't believe it." She whistled under her breath.

Like an anxious child, Hélène pulled on her seat belt until it extended a full foot in front of her. "You see, Marc..."

Then the light turned green. When Sylvie gunned the engine, the car lurched forward. The belt slipped out of Hélène's fingers, snapping at her chest like a rubber band.

"Aaaiiee!" she yelped, rubbing her smarting nipple. "He prefers eating at home."

❖

What a bizarre bird she is, thought Sylvie. Her student's clumsiness was so endearing.

Then her face turned serious as another thought entered her mind. *But anyone would be bizarre, living with that beast of a man.*

What concerned her most was Hélène's lack of adventure. As if something—or someone—had dampened her sense of curiosity. *Maybe that's why she's a closeted poet.*

"Don't you ever go out alone, or with friends?" she inquired nonchalantly.

Hélène shook her head.

"We're like complete opposites. I go out for basically every meal." Sylvie pushed harder on the accelerator. "I don't have tons of vices, but eating out sure is one of them."

Speaking of eating, I'm starved. She flattened the accelerator to the floor. "Maybe it's because I can't cook worth beans."

Hélène's eyebrows shot up. "So you're a woman of few vices?"

"What's that supposed to mean?" asked Sylvie, hitting the brakes. *Crap. Why did I say that? Red flag.* The tires screeched to a halt.

"It's just that—" began Hélène, gripping her seat.

"Appearances can be deceiving." Sylvie hit the accelerator, and the car lurched forward. "I can count mine on one hand." She lifted her hand from the wheel. "Let's see…" She uncurled each finger. "Tasty restaurants; pretty flowers; soft, romantic music; the beach; and—"

"Wait a sec. You call those vices?" Hélène chuckled. "If those are vices, then I'm full of them too, 'cause—"

"I'm not done yet. What about this one?" asked Sylvie, uncurling her last finger.

❖

Hélène's heart beat faster as she observed Sylvie's pinkie unfold. "What is it?"

"Well…" Sylvie winked at her student.

"Watch out!" yelled Hélène, pointing at a truck heading straight at them.

Sylvie swerved to the right. "*Mon Dieu,* that was close." She let out a sigh. Then, with a coquettish smile, she wiggled her pinkie. "Take a guess."

Hélène squirmed. The skin behind her neck was tingling again. *I don't like this game.* Even though downtown Brussels was a maze of narrow one-way streets, she could tell Sylvie knew all the shortcuts. Obviously, the Greek athlete relished her power behind the wheel, gunning the engine, whizzing her VW bug over the cobblestones like an insect on speed.

She reminds me of Marc, Hélène realized, digging her nails into her seat as the goddess carved tight turns around impending obstacles—cars, bikes, motorcycles, and pedestrians—like an Olympic skier.

But she's in control. Unlike Marc. She exhaled at last. *I actually feel safe with her.*

"Come on, what is it?" Sylvie's voice broke her thoughts.

"What?" Hélène looked at Sylvie's pinkie again. "I have no idea."

"What happens when you put 'em all together? Tasty restaurants, nice flowers, soft music, the beach—"

"Ah! I get it..." Giggling nervously, Hélène stuck her face out the window. *That's a vice I don't seem to have.* The breeze cooled her flushing cheeks. *Sex doesn't seem to be my forte...But maybe it's not too late.* She ran her fingers through her hair, hoping the steady stream of fresh air would give it a younger, wilder look—like Sylvie's.

❖

"We're here!" exclaimed Sylvie as she wedged her VW bug between two parked cars.

"*Bisou...*" She bumped the car in front. "*Bisou...*" She nudged the car behind.

"*Voilà!*" she exclaimed after her bug kissed the cars. With a twist of her screwdriver, she cut the engine. "Hope you're hungry, *kopela.*"

Hélène had to skip to stay abreast of Sylvie, whose long legs propelled her athletic silhouette as quickly as toothpaste oozing from a tube.

She must be starving, mused Hélène, quickening her pace...until she saw two bare feet looming ahead. *Ah non, it's him.* The homeless man was wearing the same ragged clothes he wore the day Marc had insulted him, near the market.

Hélène lowered her eyes to elude his gaze. But as soon as they approached, the man thrust a dirty hand in their direction.

"Happen to have a coin or two to spare, *Mesdames?*"

"*Eh bien,*" began Hélène, averting the man's glossy eyes. They seemed wet, like a steamy mirror after a shower. *But he hasn't had any showers for a while,* she decided, mentally blocking the stench.

Then she saw Sylvie bend down before the man and take his filthy hand in hers.

What in the heck is she doing? Hélène stiffened as the younger woman pumped his hand with a friendly smile. "*Bonjour,* Frank. How's it going?"

Hélène held her breath. *She knows him?*

The man searched Sylvie's face, then shook his head.

But Sylvie kept smiling until his jaw opened, loosening his sunbaked lips. They parted to reveal a toothless grin. "Now I recognize you, *ma fille,*" he said gruffly. His eyes grew even soggier as they lit up.

I can't believe this. Hélène felt imaginary fingers closing in on her throat, squeezing it into a knot. *I have to get out of here.* Gasping for air, she began to run…

After Sylvie and the homeless man had exchanged pleasantries, Sylvie released his hand and turned around. Hélène was gone.

She spotted her at the far end of the block, cowering under an olive tree.

"You know that guy?" asked Hélène when Sylvie finally caught up to her.

"*Qui?* Frank? Of course. He's here most days."

"And you don't mind shaking his hand?"

"*Mais non.* Why should I?"

"Because he's dirty, and he's probably—"

Sylvie crossed her arms. "I bet nobody shakes his hand. In fact, I bet nobody ever touches him."

Hélène chuckled. "You're right about that. I certainly wouldn't. You should be careful who you touch, Sylvie. Never know what kind of—"

"It's the least I can do. Show him someone cares." Sylvie's dark eyes intensified. "The poor guy's homeless. He's lost his family. It's not much, but I like to think it means something to him that I care."

As soon as Hélène heard those last two words, with that sensuous Greek accent, she aimed her eyes on the lines in the sidewalk. It was all she could do to keep herself from grabbing the goddess and hugging her with all her might.

She tried to swallow it away, but the knot in her throat tightened instead.

What a contrast to Marc, Hélène kept thinking as she walked next to Sylvie, recalling her compassionate face as she spoke to the homeless man. Her caring demeanor touched the sensitive poet's heart on a deeply emotional level. *She really feels for him. In just a few seconds, it's like she transformed him. She's not simply a swimming teacher; she's an alchemist*, Hélène decided, sneaking a peek at Sylvie's full lips as she explained the situation of the increasing homeless population in Brussels.

Hélène nodded her head and murmured "*Ah bon?* Really?" every few sentences. She kept her chin up as they walked, focusing her eyes on the dark clouds above their heads. It was all she could do to keep the tears from dribbling out.

"What in the heck are you doing?" inquired Sylvie, yanking Hélène's sleeve before she walked into a tree.

"You know I adore plants," replied Hélène with an embarrassed chuckle, discreetly wiping away a tear.

"Stick with me from now on." Sylvie pinned her student's arm under her own.

A soft, light aura surrounded the two women's figures as they strolled, elbows fused, down the street.

At last, Sylvie stopped in front of Dionysos Taverna. "Here we are."

"Looks nice," gushed Hélène, peering through the lace curtains of the blue-and-white painted building. *And so quaint.* Tiny glass vases with red tulips were nestled amongst massive plates of food on each of the blue-and-white checkered tables. The patrons—all very Greek-looking—gesticulated heavily with their hands as they devoured mysterious delicacies, washing them down with countless carafes of wine.

Ca alors! My boring sandwiches can't compare to this, Hélène mused, suddenly aware of her gurgling stomach.

"It's cozy. Especially in winter," replied Sylvie. "And it's even nicer out back. There's a garden and—"

Hélène extended her palm toward the daunting sky. "Looks like it's going to rain."

"*Ouais*, maybe. But I'm cooped up all day. It's so nice to get some fresh air, *non*?" Sylvie flashed her a persuasive smile. "And I spend most of my waking hours in the water. So if you think a little moisture in the sky can chase me away, you don't know me very well."

Hélène blushed. "*Non.* Guess I don't."

"And now that you're a swimmer, you should start thinking like this too. Life's too short to—"

"Guess I didn't realize." Hélène nodded bashfully. "*D'accord*, lead the way."

"Follow me," said Sylvie with a wink. She led her past a stream of gregarious diners digging into steaming plates of food. Forks plunged into lamb kebabs. Hearty laughs chased long gulps of white wine.

Hélène couldn't fathom what the diners were saying, but their vibrant intonation, the way the syllables bunched together—bouncing one "th" off another, and ending with either an "ia" or an "io"—rendered Greek the liveliest, most musical language she had ever heard. *Latin may be long dead, but Greek is as alive as ever*, she mused.

"Through here," said Sylvie, grabbing Hélène's hand.

Hélène shuddered at the touch of her firm grip. Then she noticed two elderly men seated at a back table. One hollered to Sylvie in Greek. The other whispered something to him; both men started laughing.

Ignoring them, Sylvie pushed open a wooden blue door.

Hélène glanced back at the men. The mustached one yelled something to her in Greek. *Wonder what he's saying?* Shrugging, she followed Sylvie outdoors. Even after they penetrated the lush garden, the enticing aroma of foreign spices and grilled meat lingered in the air.

❖

"Looks like we've got the place to ourselves," whispered Sylvie, approaching a petite iron table wedged in the back, next to a red brick wall. A lofty tree with gnarled branches sprouting tiny white flowers made this spot the most intimate in the garden amongst all the empty tables.

Like a well-groomed gentleman, Sylvie pulled back a chair for Hélène. Then she plopped down next to her.

Hélène stiffened as she felt Sylvie's body unusually close. Their shoulders were nearly touching. Pretending she didn't notice, Hélène aimed her nose at the delicate white flowers dangling above their heads and took a deep whiff. *Honeysuckle. So sweet, just like this moment.*

Sylvie leaned closer and whispered as if someone could

overhear her. "It's so stuffy inside, *je déteste*. Especially at lunchtime."

Hélène nodded. "Do you know everyone in there?"

"Of course. We all know each other somehow," Sylvie said with a sigh. "The Greek community here is like one huge family. Dysfunctional, to be sure, but still a family. It's a cultural thing." She paused to take in the beauty of the verdant garden.

"We're not as reserved as you Belgians. And the older men...*Eh bien*, they can get really obnoxious at times. Especially after they've knocked back a few glasses."

"I don't mind," Hélène was quick to comment. "I didn't get a word they were saying. Actually, it's kind of exotic." Hélène bit down on her lip. *Like you. I wonder what you're like after you've knocked back a few.*

Sylvie snickered. "Sometimes I think you're too nice for your own good. You've got to learn to protect yourself." She squeezed Hélène's arm. "Especially since you're a poet."

Hélène felt the tiny hairs at the back of her neck bristle. Sylvie's hand was still gripping her arm. "Poet? Ha!" she exclaimed, careful not to budge, lest Sylvie remove her hand. She held her breath, feeling Sylvie's energy radiating through her thick sweater, penetrating her skin. The tingling spread from her arm and raced down her side, heading toward her thigh. "Anyway, sure smells good in there," she stammered.

"Just wait till you taste it." Sylvie gave her a squeeze, licking her sensuous lips. "This is by far the best Greek restaurant in Brussels. And I should know. I've tried every single one of them."

❖

Hélène knew she should be at work or home in bed, but for some inexplicable reason, she didn't feel guilty. Guilt wasn't what was bothering her, it was something deeper, more…As her mind searched for the precise word, her blue eyes drifted up to the faded parasol, nestled amongst the twisted branches and delicate white flowers, perched like a dainty mushroom over the two women's heads.

Sylvie leaned over and broke the silence. "Cozy here, *n'est-ce pas*?"

Hélène sat up abruptly, wincing at the hard iron rods under her thin chair cushion. "*Oui*. It's exquisite."

Sylvie leaned even closer. "I'm so glad you stopped by the pool. What a surprise, finding you on the grass. What kinds of poems were you writing, anyway?"

Hélène pretended to study the bark of a nearby tree. "What? Nothing, really."

"Come on. It didn't look like 'nothing.' You were burning up the pages. Do you always write like that?"

Hélène grimaced. "I was just jotting down a couple of ideas—"

"A couple of ideas, *mon œil*! Despite all appearances, I bet you lead an exciting life." Sylvie chuckled, peering into Hélène's wide eyes. "Maybe you're a double agent?"

Now it was Hélène's turn to laugh. "Just a boring translator. Sorry to disappoint you."

"*Alors*, in that little book of yours…no dark secrets lurking about?"

Hélène felt her cheeks growing hot. "Not that I know of." She cleared her throat.

Sylvie's eyes were sparkling. Before Hélène could stop her, she reached over. "Let's see what's in here!"

Hélène intercepted before she could get into her bag. "Hey, you can't just—"

"Ah, yes, I can!" Sylvie's shoulder dug into Hélène's chest. "I'm your teacher, so you have to obey me!" The two women formed a tangled ball of limbs as they struggled against each other. The closeness of their bodies made Hélène dizzy. The smell of chlorine on Sylvie's skin drew her in. So familiar. *So sexy.*

Before Hélène knew what was happening, a hot feeling shot through her body. Pleasure mingling with pain, like a sharp elbow nudging her consciousness, poked her in all the tender spots. *What do I do now?*

Hélène braced herself as Sylvie's breath caressed her cheeks.

Chapter Sixteen

Vassilios, the waiter, entered the garden carrying a basket of fresh pita bread, two menus, and a large plate of Kalamata olives. He was whistling a Greek tune, but as soon as he saw the table in the far corner, he stopped. *She'll never change*, he concluded, shaking his head.

He lit a cigarette and stood on the porch, watching. After all, it wasn't every day that he could observe two sexy women grabbing at each other in the garden.

Sylvie's arm was arched high in the air, ready to swoop into the other woman's bag. Her prominent nose was an inch away from Hélène's. Vassilios could imagine Sylvie's warm breath falling on the blond woman's lips, her dark eyes boring into the other's—about to devour her.

Vassilios took another drag on his cigarette. The seconds ticked by until the other woman poked Sylvie in the boob.

"Aaaiieee!" shrieked Sylvie, rubbing her breast as she pulled away.

Vassilios cupped his hand over his mouth to conceal a jubilant snort. *Good for you, pitsirika. Time someone taught her a lesson.*

❖

With a flustered face, Hélène stammered, "Sorry, but my diary's private. I don't show it to anyone."

"So it's a diary." Sylvie maintained her grip on Hélène's arm. "Not even your husband?"

"You kidding?" Hélène's eyes went ablaze. "That would be suicide."

"Fine. But I'm not your husband." Sylvie lunged toward Hélène's bag again.

"It's full of personal stuff. Just stupid ideas. I'd die if someone read it," retorted Hélène, clutching her bag and turning away.

"Never mind. We're not here to fight. I brought you here to eat, remember?"

As soon as the words left Sylvie's mouth, Hélène swung around. "Now you're talking."

Sylvie yelled something in Greek. Vassilios stubbed out his cigarette with his shoe and dashed over.

As soon as Hélène saw Vassilios, her body went stiff. The waiter looked more like a Greek statue than a person. He flashed them a gallant smile, but all Hélène noticed were his beefy pectoral muscles protruding from his open shirt. She could almost smell the testosterone in the air.

Vassilios dumped the basket of pita bread and olives on the table and—with his well-defined lips—planted affectionate kisses on Sylvie's cheeks.

Only a half inch from her lips, Hélène calculated. Her stomach began to rumble. When the waiter draped a bushy arm over Sylvie's shoulder and whispered something in Greek into her ear, Hélène gripped her chair with angst. *I wonder if Sylvie likes hairy chests?* She tried to tear her eyes away from the pair but couldn't.

He's looking at her like she's his supper. Hélène pinched her lips together to fight off a scowl.

"So, what have we dragged in from the sea today?" he aked in perfect French, with hardly an accent. Winking at Sylvie, he added something in Greek with lots of th's and io's.

Hélène felt stupid for not understanding. She knew they were talking about her. And she was a translator—her job was to detect what other people said. Hélène offered him a saccharine gaze. *Why can't he just act like a normal waiter and drop off the menus?* Hélène took in a deep breath to swallow her irritation.

"So, what are you in the mood for?" Sylvie asked abruptly, pointing to the menu.

Hélène blinked twice. All the writing was in incomprehensible Greek characters. "This place certainly is authentic. Whatever you like is fine with me."

"*Non*, really. What are your favorite dishes?"

Hélène squirmed. "Actually, um, I've never tasted Greek food before."

"You're kidding, right?" Sylvie looked at Vassilios, who raised a bushy brow. Hélène sunk deeper in her chair.

"Well, you're in for a real treat. Let's start with some *mezé*." The goddess continued in Greek, "A *mezé* for two and a half liter of retsina. Thanks, Vassili."

The waiter jutted his decisive chin at the two women, winked at Sylvie, and left.

Hélène forced a smile at Sylvie. "So you really *are* Greek. I wasn't sure," she stammered. "You hardly have an accent."

"Really? Are you trying to butter me up? I'm one hundred percent Greek—nutritiously grown on the island of Santorini." Sylvie pointed to her prominent nose. "See this? It's sculpted just like a Greek statue. We've kept this nose in our family for centuries!"

"Santorini? *Vraiment?*" Hélène reached into her bag. "Look." She handed her the small oil painting.

Sylvie examined it with interest. "Where'd you get this?"

Hélène blushed. "I've got my connections."

"It says 'Santorini 1983.' Wonder who painted it?"

"There's no name on it."

"Look, you can even see my house," Sylvie gushed.

"Which one?"

"The white one on top of the cliff."

"But they're all white," Hélène said, feeling her anxiety melt as soon as Sylvie chortled along with her.

"Here. *Tiens.*" Sylvie's chocolate-colored eyes were glistening.

"*Non*, you can keep it."

"That's sweet of you, but I don't need it. I've got the *real* Santorini locked in here." Sylvie put her hand on her heart. "Take it," she insisted, handing the picture back.

"Now, try some retsina," Sylvie prodded, filling Hélène's glass with the pale-yellow liquid. Hélène held up her glass and sniffed.

"Smells like Chanel No. 7," she declared, scrunching her nose.

"I'll take that as a compliment," Sylvie cooed. "Drink up, it's good for you."

Hélène pinched her nose and tried a small sip, averting her gaze from Sylvie's luscious eyes.

"So?"

"Nice," muttered Hélène. Not only did it reek of Chanel No. 7, it tasted like it. *This stuff is lethal*, she mused, swirling the yellow liquid in her glass.

❖

While waiting for their food, the two women chatted casually—until Hélène popped the question that had been eating at her for weeks. "Why isn't your name Greek?" she blurted.

"Because it's not my real name."

Hélène's ears perked.

Sylvie leaned forward. "My grandpa traveled a lot, you see. He settled in France after World War Two. In fact, he traveled so much, and his name was so hard to pronounce, that finally, everyone just ended up calling him Routard." She inserted an olive into her mouth, then skewered one for Hélène with her toothpick.

"Home-grown," she offered with a tempting grin.

Hélène shook her head. "*S'il te plaît*, continue…"

"Your loss," murmured Sylvie, munching on the olive before resuming her story. "So when I moved to Belgium at age nineteen, I decided to use that name too. I admired my grandpa so much, you see." She spat out her olive pit.

Vassilios deftly unloaded an armful of aromatic, spicy dishes on their table.

"After a full morning of swimming lessons, I'm famished." Sylvie heaped an assortment of *mezé* onto Hélène's plate, then loaded up her own. "*Kalí óreksi…*I mean *bon appétit*," she added, digging into her food. "*Mmm*, I adore this stuff."

Hélène watched with wide eyes as Sylvie ingested three times as much as she did. *Incroyable. I've never seen a woman take in so much food in one sitting.* As for her own appetite, nibbling was the only way to thwart the nausea still lurking in her system. She tried to conceal her uneasiness by wrestling with her fork: rearranging the vine leaves, Kalamata olives, fried squid curls, and unidentified pink-and-white creamy paste gracing her plate.

Whatever this all is, it must be delicious, she concluded, witnessing the expression of ecstasy on Sylvie's face. These savory, calorie-filled wonders might look and smell like heaven; unfortunately, they wreaked havoc on Hélène's queasy intestines after her junk-food binge. To her relief, Sylvie had no qualms about helping her polish off her lunch.

Hélène watched with amusement as Sylvie wrapped the warm pita bread around her fingers and sponged all the excess sauce from Hélène's plate. Then, ever so slowly, Sylvie brought the pita bread to her luscious lips. They gently parted to expose Sylvie's white teeth while her tongue ventured out, licking her plump bottom lip.

Hélène watched mutely as Sylvie's mouth opened just wide enough for her to take a generous bite from the lavishly smothered thin bread. *She's not kidding. She really digs this stuff.* Hélène noticed a small trickle of yogurt, garlic, and dill sauce drip onto Sylvie's muscular wrist. *That wrist. That arm.* Hélène's thoughts went back to the car, and Sylvie's strong forearms as she deftly maneuvered the steering wheel. *She's a sexy driver and a sexy eater. Men must go nuts over her...I'm starting to go crazy myself.*

To make up for her quasi-anorexic behavior, Hélène made an effort with the ghastly white wine. After a few swigs, she realized as long as she blocked her nose—ever so subtly—she could get the liquid down. It was just a matter of keeping it there.

"*Tiens*, let me help you," Sylvie cooed, inching closer to Hélène. She extended her index finger and painted Hélène's lips with retsina. "Just pretend it's a new shade of lipstick."

Sylvie's finger traced the contours of Hélène's lips, moistening them, lingering.

Hélène felt tiny goose bumps rise on her arms. "Greek gloss," she whispered with a self-conscious grin.

Both wineglasses were empty. Giddy from their Greek gastronomical orgy, the women simply gazed at each other.

Temporarily suspended in an intimate, floating bubble, they lost all notion of time. Hélène peered into Sylvie's dark eyes, which seemed to lure her in, ready to swallow her whole.

At last, Hélène tore her eyes away. *That was intense.* She folded her blue napkin. *"C'était délicieux!* Thanks for bringing me here. It's so nice to be on dry land with you, for once."

Sylvie responded with a throaty laugh. "Yes, it is. And I'm glad you liked the culinary adventure. Come with me whenever you want. *Tiens,* aren't those new glasses?"

Hélène blushed. *"Ouais."*

"Let's see." Sylvie plucked the glasses from Hélène's face. She leaned toward Hélène until their eyes were two inches apart. "Much better. Now I can see your luscious blue eyes."

Hélène shivered at the closeness of their bodies; she could still smell the chlorine on Sylvie's skin. *She thinks my eyes are luscious?* A barrage of conflicting thoughts swept into her mind until Sylvie abruptly pulled away and returned her glasses.

"They're almost as sexy as your diving mask." Sylvie punched her lightly on the shoulder.

"Hey, you're my teacher. You're not allowed to tease me."

"Sorry." Sylvie let out a hiccup. "I'll just take your picture instead." She dug into her backpack for her camera.

"Ah, non!" Hélène covered her face. She had never liked having her picture taken. The last thing she wanted right now was a permanent image of herself captured by Sylvie. She could feel her cheeks blushing at the thought of her secret—the pair of them frittering away the afternoon in this secluded garden paradise. Instead of safely translating at her office, she was downing glasses of stinky Greek wine while rubbing elbows—and perhaps more—with her attractive swimming

coach. She squeezed her eyes shut as she licked the last taste of retsina from her lips. *I wish I could just disappear.*

"You look great. It's a real Kodak moment." Gently, Sylvie pulled Hélène's hands from her face.

"But I don't like—"

"Vassilios can take our picture. Want an espresso?"

"*Non, merci.* I already had my caffeine fix this morning." Hélène winced. "You go ahead."

"I'll be right back." Sylvie jumped up.

Hélène checked her instructor out as she crossed the garden. *I love how she walks. So carefree and casual, yet so graceful.* Sylvie's strong legs propelled her body forward, followed by her tight, muscular buttocks. *Those are amazing jeans.* Hélène tingled all over, realizing how attracted she was to this androgynous, sexy woman. She held her breath. *What's coming next?*

❖

"Which button do I push?" the waiter asked with a frown.

"Come on, Vassili. What do you think this is, an automatic?" Sylvie chuckled. "You know me better than that. I'm a manual kind of—"

"*Ah oui*, I'm sure you are, *ma chérie*. I bet nobody's as manual as—"

Sylvie's nostrils flared. "Here, let me adjust it for you." Grabbing the camera, she focused the lens on Hélène. "Give us a big smile."

Hélène forced her lips into a lukewarm smirk.

"*Non*, I want a real one. Show us your teeth!"

Even though Hélène felt vulnerable before the camera, her attitude softened at Sylvie's candid enthusiasm. Her tingle of attraction was still there. *What wouldn't I do to please her?* Cranking open her mouth, Hélène exposed her choppers to the sky.

"Much better." Sylvie snapped the shutter, then handed her camera to Vassilios.

"Looks good, *mesdames*, but you need to squeeze together," he ordered. "Come on, a bit closer now."

The two women narrowed the gap between their bodies and Sylvie promptly wrapped her arm around Hélène. As soon as Hélène felt the goddess's solid shoulder against her chest, a rush of adrenaline hit her.

Vassilios lowered the camera and whispered to Hélène. "*Mon ange*, you really must try to look less constipated. Now, relax and smile for the camera."

Sylvie shot him an exasperated look, while Hélène's lips tightened. "Constipated" was hardly her favorite word, especially when it described her face. But for Sylvie's sake, she forced herself to relax.

"At least I got your heads." The waiter chuckled after four attempts. "Or somewhere in the vicinity."

Sylvie shot him a sharp response in Greek.

Vassilios laughed all the way back to the restaurant.

"Sorry about that," muttered Sylvie. "He can be so annoying sometimes. His big dream was to go to Broadway and…"

But Hélène wasn't listening; her mind was too busy analyzing. *They sure seem intimate. Maybe an ex-couple?* She didn't really want to know.

Then again, yes she did. She couldn't help imagining her swimming instructor's nimble fingers pulling on the thick leather belt holding up his white sailor pants, slowly undoing it…

She imagined Sylvie's teeth on the silver buckle. *Non!*

Wiping the sweat from her forehead, Hélène glanced at Sylvie's full lips, which were still rambling with the effects of the potent Greek wine.

Then Sylvie's expression turned serious. "*Ca va?* You don't look so good."

Is it that obvious? wondered Hélène, tapping her moist cheeks. "It's just the wine. I'm not used to having alcohol at lunch."

Sylvie chuckled. "Well then, *mea culpa*." She reached toward Hélène and swept a strand of shiny hair behind her ear. "I must be a bad influence on you."

"*Non.* You're not."

"Not yet, perhaps." Sylvie's dark eyes sparkled. "Anyway, have you decided about the lessons? If we do it on Saturdays, we won't have the pool to ourselves anymore, but..."

Not yet, perhaps...What's that supposed to mean? Hélène wondered, feeling the tingle rush between her legs. *Focus... focus.* Her eyes narrowed in on Sylvie's hands, which were gesticulating in the air. Her fingers were long, and strong, like the rest of her body. Hélène's imagination took over, making her dizzy, generating a rush of unsettling thoughts, full of hot, graphic images of the two of them in terribly intimate poses.

This potent concoction—mixed with a half liter of retsina—swished in Hélène's brain. She squeezed her eyes hard to block it out.

"So what do you say?" asked Sylvie, concluding her monologue. "About Saturday lessons."

Hélène mutely stared at the Greek goddess, amazed to be still sitting on her chair.

❖

After several moments of confusion, the answer came to Hélène: *Screw Marc.*

"Let's do it!" she blurted.

"*Super.* I'll ask the director tomorrow, then. We can start next Saturday. At eight sharp."

Hélène's eyebrows shot up. Sylvie seemed genuinely excited at the idea of rising early on Saturdays to give her lessons.

As if to confirm her thoughts, Sylvie added, "I really enjoy our lessons, you know."

Hélène felt a rush of heat hit her cheeks. "Me too. It's bizarre, I always hated the water. That's why I avoided it all these years. What a waste!"

"How could anyone hate water?" Sylvie peered at her. "I thrive in it."

A vivid image popped into Hélène's mind. Her teacher emerged halfway out of the pool, flicking her wet hair from her shoulders. A stream of droplets landed on Hélène's face. The two women laughed, moist breasts jiggling, before joining to embrace.

Cupping her water glass, Hélène held her breath as she generated slow circles on the table. The swirling water licked at the sides like tiny waves at the beach. "I know," she purred. "It feels heavenly—my entire being vibrates as soon as I'm in the pool. Does yours too?"

"That depends," said Sylvie, peering at the pulsating water.

"On what?" Hélène dug her fingernails into the glass.

Sylvie lifted her chocolate eyes. "On whom I'm with," she answered with a playful wink.

Hélène blushed again, realizing that she had just been extended an invitation. This intimate conversation went well beyond simply flirting. *What do I do now? If she were a guy, I'd probably clear out of here.* She glanced at the empty garden tables in a desperate attempt to calm her racing thoughts. *But she's not a guy. And she is so damn cute. And sexy. And nobody's around.*

"*Excuse-moi.*" Before Hélène could stop herself, she bent down and untied her right boot. "Where were we?" she asked with a sly grin, extending her bare toes under the table.

The surprise on her face was worth it. "*Mon Dieu!*" Sylvie exclaimed.

Hélène shrugged. "My toes were cold, so I thought you might warm them…It's working."

Sylvie pinched her lips. "Ahem. Do you always do this when you dine with friends?"

Hélène laughed heartily. "First of all, I never dine out. Remember?" She leaned closer. "And we're not actually friends, *n'est-ce pas?*"

Sylvie paused.

Hélène could feel the tingling in her toes as they rubbed Sylvie's ankle. Indeed, they were warmer now.

Sylvie's dark eyes grew glossy with emotion. She remained silent.

She's enjoying this. Encouraged, Hélène traced her big toe along the inside of Sylvie's calf, savoring the roughness of her teacher's jeans.

"We're not actually friends, *n'est-ce pas?*" Hélène repeated, drumming up her most sexy, guttural tone as she moved her toe upward toward Sylvie's thigh.

"I'm your instructor, and you're…" Sylvie started to reply in a strained voice.

"You know what I mean. You feel the attraction between us as much as I do, don't you?" Hélène surprised herself with her newfound expression of confidence. Without waiting for a response, she rubbed her toe against Sylvie's inner thigh and peered into her eyes. "We could be much more." Rather than dissuading her, the startled look on Sylvie's face excited Hélène. She wanted more, and she desperately hoped her instructor did too. Her heartbeat quickened as the seconds ticked by.

"Of course I do," Sylvie finally replied, leveling her voice. "But let's face it, you're married. You may not be happy in your marriage, but you're still married. I've done this charade before. *C'est impossible.* Believe me, it never works out. Everyone gets hurt in the end." Sylvie removed Hélène's foot from her lap.

"But Marc's cheating on me," Hélène spat out, suddenly realizing the truth.

He had never admitted it, but she knew deep down he had a lover. A long-term lover. And she'd never even had the guts to confront him about it. She cringed when she recalled his reaction a few nights before when Marc noticed her new haircut.

She had wanted to surprise him with a romantic dinner in their garden, but all his attention had focused on her hair.

"Must have cost you a bundle. What a waste of money," he had yelled, insulting her.

Hélène's cheeks had been burning. *It's none of your business how much I paid. How about adding up all you spend on the gym, car racing, computers, season tickets to soccer games...* Rampant thoughts had raced through her mind. *A heck of a lot more than a haircut!*

She had been tempted to recite the list, but the cool air on her skin reminded her they were outside, within earshot of all the neighbors. So she had swallowed her anger—again.

And now, she realized, *all those late nights. All those trips to the gym. It didn't really matter. Nothing really mattered in my life. Until now. I've got to call Ceci to tell her she was right. She was right about everything...*

"*Vraiment?*" Sylvie asked, raising her eyes. "Why didn't you tell me before?"

"Because I didn't realize it until now. But I don't care. What I *do* care about is us. You and me. I can't think of anything but you. Ever since the first day we met at the market, and I found your keychain, remember? And then we met again at the pool. *Ce n'était pas un hazard.* This is more than pure coincidence. It's fate. We were meant to be together. Please, Sylvie, just give us a chance."

When Hélène squeezed Sylvie's hand, she felt a jolt of electricity sizzle through their fingers.

"Coffee's here!" announced Vassilios, creeping up on the two women. Promptly, he draped an arm around Sylvie's shoulder while delivering her a minuscule cup of espresso.

Hélène couldn't help noticing the way his arm touched Sylvie's breast—and lingered there.

So maybe they're bosom buddies. But he doesn't have to take the term literally!

Agonizing stomach cramps ensued...until a rebellious burp exploded from Hélène's lips. Horrified, Hélène cupped her mouth. "*Excusez-moi!*"

Between guffaws, Vassilios blurted, "Sounds like your *kopela* liked the meal, Syl!"

Hélène's eyes were stinging with tears—but not from laughter. Clutching her stomach, she abruptly stood.

"*Skáse*, you idiot!" hissed Sylvie in Greek. "Can't you see she's upset? You're just making things worse."

The waiter excused himself profusely and left.

"Please sit down." Sylvie motioned to Hélène. "Sorry he's such a brute. No manners at all."

Silence reigned as the two women sat side by side in the

quaint garden setting. The lush atmosphere reminded Hélène of her latest poem, provoking a deep sense of peace in her—with the exception of a certain lingering thought: *I'm obsessed with her.*

She observed Sylvie's strong fingers stir several spoonfuls of sugar into her tiny espresso, then bring the beverage to her sensuous lips. Hélène caught a glimpse of Sylvie's pink tongue as her lips parted; she took the rim of her cup in her mouth and sucked down the sweet, thick liquid. Then she turned to face Hélène, licking her moist lips.

"Delicious," Sylvie stated in a raspy voice. She held her spoon—coated with sugar and bitter coffee granules—up to Hélène's lips and peered into her eyes. "Want a taste?"

Chapter Seventeen

Dozens of dark clouds hung over the two women as they left the restaurant. Hélène felt raw, exposed, even guilty after her confession to Sylvie. She knew she shouldn't have come to lunch with her. She should be at the office translating, not wasting her time with this woman. What terrible bug had bitten her, to make her think this would work out?

I must have a fever. I must be sick. Her hand went to her forehead. It was warm and sticky. *I sure am sick. Sick of this whole messed-up situation. I want my life to go back to normal.* She felt her heart beat wildly under her blouse. *But what is normal? I just want to go home.* She quickened her step.

Ahead on the sidewalk, Frank, the homeless man, sat with his chin on his chest, bare feet splayed.

Hélène approached him like a steamroller, and cleared her throat.

As soon as his swollen eyes noticed her, he stuck out his palm. "Would you happen to have a coin or two to—"

"*Voici.*" Hélène shoved a €20 bill into his dirty hand.

Frank's eyes bulged.

"It's not much, but I hope it helps."

The homeless man held the bill an inch from his eyes. "*Merci, Madame.*"

"Get yourself some shoes," ordered Hélène, marching off with Sylvie on her heels.

When they reached the VW bug, Sylvie touched Hélène's arm. "Listen…" she began.

Hélène shook it off. "*Non.* You listen. I'm sorry you're not interested in me. I guess I'm not good enough for you. Or sexy enough. Or young enough." She exhaled forcefully. "I'll just grab a cab…"

"*Skatá!* Over my dead body!" cursed Sylvie in Greek, crossing herself. "What is wrong with you, woman?"

The black sky stretched over the pair, its obscure canvas riddled with ominous slivers of lightning. Hélène glanced at the rain clouds, wishing she knew the answer herself. *What the heck is wrong with me?*

The mood in the car was as cozy as a soggy woolen blanket.

Hélène kept her gaze on the road during every painful second with Sylvie, squinting behind her glasses to keep her tears from spilling out. She wished someone would thrust a wall between them, to separate her from this person who could make her feel so great one minute, yet so dreadful the next. Just like the bitter coffee granules mixed with sweet sugar lingering on her tongue. She glanced at Sylvie's arms as she maneuvered the car, her well-defined forearm muscles flexing as she gripped the wheel.

Hélène's stomach lurched at a sharp left turn. *It's all her fault. She's like a magnet.* Despite her will to do the contrary, she studied the tiny hairs on Sylvie's tan arms, leading up to slightly bulging biceps under her T-shirt. These weren't the only things bulging under her T-shirt. Hélène gulped to keep the guilty feelings down, tormented at how she had always been attracted to light cotton on dark skin.

Maman would definitely hate her. She's a bad influence.
The air in the VW bug suddenly tasted stale.

❖

Sylvie rolled down her window. The cool breeze caressed her clammy skin. *It's going to rain any second*, she concluded, observing the black clouds overhead as she drove down busy avenues. *Maybe she has mental problems. Or she's got writer's block? It sure didn't look like it a few hours ago... Or maybe she's like most Belgians and can't take it when it rains in summer.* She thought about all the possible reasons why Hélène became so upset after their lunch, but nothing seemed plausible. *Was it because I removed her foot from my thigh? What was she thinking anyway? In a public place? At my favorite restaurant, for the world to see?* Clenching her teeth, she racked her brain to think of something to say to alleviate the unbearable silence between them.

This should lighten her up. She switched on the radio. As soft rock filled the car, Sylvie glanced at her passenger, whose lips were still pinched together, tight as clothespins.

At the next red light, Sylvie propelled a silent prayer to the sky. Instantly, the dark clouds retorted with bloated raindrops, splattering on her windshield. *This is pure agony.*

At last Sylvie reached the pool parking lot. But before she cut the engine, Hélène jumped out of the car.

"Thanks for the meal," Hélène said through the window.

"My pleasure," Sylvie replied, forcing a smile.

The splat of raindrops hitting the windshield merged with the soft rock music. When Sylvie put the engine to rest, all went silent, except the rhythmic pattering on glass.

"I'll drive you home. It's starting to pour."

Hélène stood erect in the rain, wide-eyed and confused as a stray cat mid-street. "No thanks," she replied, shaking her head vehemently.

"*M'enfin*, Hélène," countered Sylvie, as hundreds of droplets sprayed from the tips of Hélène's hair. "Don't be ridiculous. I can't let you—"

"Now that I like water…I might as well soak in it, *n'est-ce pas?*" Hélène snickered, raising her hands to the rain clouds. "Besides, it'll cool me off."

Sylvie furrowed her thick eyebrows. *This isn't like her at all.* Then she recalled an article she once read, about a young boy who went berserk after drinking a grape soda. Apparently, the artificial flavors caused certain food allergies, which radically affected his behavior. He was acting like a monster until his parents finally took him to an allergy specialist.

Images of Hélène ingesting glassfuls of retsina flashed through Sylvie's mind. *Merde. I should've taken her to a Belgian restaurant.*

But Sylvie didn't know any. She always ate Greek. "I don't mind taking you home. *Vraiment,*" she insisted.

"*Non,* thanks anyway." Hélène lessened her frown for a nanosecond as she took a wary step around a puddle.

"Okay, but be careful. I want to see you at the pool tomorrow in one piece."

When her VW bug rounded the corner, Sylvie glanced through the rearview mirror at Hélène, who was unlocking her bike. She seemed so vulnerable, bent over like a bug in the pouring rain.

As Sylvie drove away, she realized how little she understood humans—especially women. *Cats are so much easier,* she reminded herself, impatient to snuggle with Goldie on the sofa.

CHAPTER EIGHTEEN

Lying on the sofa that rainy afternoon, Hélène tried to push everything out of her mind. She had Chaussette on her stomach and a steaming mug of peppermint tea by her side. This comforting remedy would fix all ailments. It had worked in the past. But to her distress, every time she closed her eyes, she saw vivid images of Sylvie holding her tightly in the pool.

It can't work, she tried to tell herself, ignoring her racing heart. But something deep inside didn't want to believe this. Something wanted her to relish the warmth of their physical and emotional closeness. She remembered the intimacy she felt during her ride in Sylvie's car toward the Greek restaurant just a few hours earlier. How drawn she was to her. Even her messiness, somehow, was sexy. And her voracious appetite. The way she hummed as she devoured that exotic food, licked the garlic sauce off her lips, and downed that nasty wine. She remembered squirming while her bare toes explored Sylvie's inner thigh and the roughness of her jeans under the table. The ginger caresses certainly warmed them up, along with the delicious surprise on Sylvie's face.

Ever so gradually, sensual thoughts invaded Hélène's body. As she lay on the sofa with her cat on her stomach, inhaling the aroma of steeping peppermint leaves, tingling spread from the tips of her toes to her soft lips. Soon, the tingling intensified, rousing her senses, igniting her skin, wetting her tongue. It swept to her fingers, and then down again, to the tender spot between her thighs. Her eyelids fluttered like dizzy butterflies as she struggled to control her body, which—to her amazement—appeared to be morphing into a new life of its own.

❖

After their early-morning lesson, Sylvie proposed a truce. "It's Saturday. Let's take advantage of this beautiful summer day. Let's test your swimming talents in the ocean."

Hélène tightened her bath towel around her wet body and glanced out the locker room window. Sunlight filtered through the trees, indicating an unusually sunny morning. It would be a waste not to take advantage of it. And Marc was taking care of the weekly shopping; then he'd go to the market café and knock back a couple of beers. Next, he'd watch the game on TV. He wouldn't miss her. She was sure of it.

Thank goodness Ceci had convinced her last night that she was right, making Marc take responsibility for their groceries for once. Especially since he was most likely cheating on her. She didn't care anymore. They had had a deep conversation, where she'd explained to Ceci why she'd left the office early yesterday and where she'd gone with Sylvie. She'd, of course, left out the juicy part about her exploring toes under the table, but she'd shared with her best friend about her hidden feelings for a woman—her attraction to Sylvie.

To Hélène's surprise, Ceci had accepted her confession and encouraged her to follow her feminine intuition. "True love only happens once in a lifetime, *ma chérie*, and let me tell you, you haven't found it with Marc. So what are you waiting for? Follow your heart!"

Hélène smiled shyly at Sylvie and nodded "yes" to her invitation. Before she knew it, they were driving through the Belgian countryside. Lazy sheep and pastures flew by as Sylvie's old VW sped down the deserted winding roads. Hélène felt her heart pumping faster as she rubbed Sylvie's keychain between her fingers.

All of a sudden, Sylvie turned to Hélène, winked at her, and sped up to one hundred forty kilometers per hour. The two acted like carefree and rambunctious teenagers sneaking out on their first road trip. A silent complicity united them as they flew through the countryside.

When Sylvie turned on the stereo, modern Greek tunes blared from the speakers, prompting Sylvie to dance in her seat as she steered. Hélène tried to imitate her teacher's sexy movements. She stuck her arms and head out the window and, breathing in the fresh air, she yelled like a wild hyena.

As the couple advanced through the lush, green landscape, they guzzled down cans of diet soda. Hélène threw popcorn at Sylvie as they whizzed past cows, pigs, horses, prairies, fields, flowers, forests, and quaint villages. The sun floated high in the cloudless azure sky.

When they finally arrived at the Belgian coast, Sylvie parked her car next to the deserted dunes. Opening the trunk, she pulled out a checkered wool blanket, a picnic basket, a bottle of red wine, and a loaf of French bread. She handed Hélène a boom box and flipped on the switch. The pair skipped to earsplitting music as they approached the sandy dunes.

At last, Sylvie led Hélène to a secluded spot where the sparkling sea stretched before their eyes. Its bold blueness contrasted with the sand's crisp whiteness. Sylvie spread out the picnic blanket, then started taking off her jeans. Hélène's jaw dropped as she watched. *Mon Dieu. What is she doing?*

Sylvie took off her shirt. *C'est pas possible.* Hélène's heart jumped a beat. She glanced at the empty dunes surrounding them. As soon as Sylvie was down to a pair of tiny black panties, Hélène cut the radio and stammered, "Wha...What are you doing?"

Sylvie grinned. "What does it look like? We're going swimming."

"Out there?" Hélène gulped at the waves crashing in the distance.

"*Non*, in the pool...Of course out there!" Sylvie approached her. "Don't tell me you're scared?"

A wave of panic hit Hélène. It was panic mingled with anticipated pleasure. Sylvie was the most attractive woman she had ever seen in her life. And there she was, standing a foot away, wearing tiny black panties and nothing else. The nipples on her firm breasts were pointing straight at Hélène. The two women stood secluded between sand dunes at an empty beach. Hélène looked at Sylvie's strong, sexy body with its smooth, tan skin. She watched her wavy, dark hair blow in the wind. She looked just like a model or, as Hélène had continually thought, a Greek goddess. Hélène became conscious of her own pale body and cringed. Even though she had recently lost a lot of weight and replaced excess fat with muscle, firming her body in all the right places, her old self-conscious doubts returned. She crossed her arms. "I've never swum in the ocean. Besides, I didn't bring my suit."

"That isn't stopping me. Don't be a chicken!" Sylvie grabbed Hélène's arm.

Hélène resisted. "*Non*, you go ahead. Someone's got to stay here and watch our stuff."

"But nobody's around!" Sylvie grimaced. "Don't be such

a prude, Hélène. *On y va!*" Ducking behind Hélène, she forced her to stand.

"That's not it," Hélène protested, feeling Sylvie's arms around her waist. "It's just…"

Sylvie snuck her head behind her ear and whispered in a husky voice: "Don't forget, I'm a lifeguard. If you start to drown, I'll save you."

"That's what I'm worried about." Hélène felt a delicious shudder at the thought of Sylvie's muscular arms pressing against her body, her cool lips on hers, resuscitating her.

Sylvie gently turned Hélène around. "What did you say?" she asked, gazing into her eyes.

"*Eh bien*…I can't believe you're making me do this." Hélène sighed as she slowly removed her blouse, revealing a baggy white T-shirt underneath. *If I had known we were doing this today, I would've worn a nicer shirt.* Embarrassed, she could feel Sylvie's eyes penetrate her entire body as she unbuttoned her jeans. She quickly slid them off and—like a shy little child—gazed at her teacher. As she did this, Hélène noticed how her feelings toward her body had changed since she had started exercising and dieting. She was much more mindful now, and more confident. She could feel how her muscles made her stronger. Never before would she have shed her clothes to expose her vulnerability outdoors—in such an intimate way—with a woman. The realization brought her a shiver of excitement. She narrowed her eyes at Sylvie, who stood in the sand with her arms on her hips, grinning. Hélène could feel her T-shirt floating like a sail over her bare thighs. "Let's get this over with," she grumbled, diverting her eyes toward the ocean.

"Haven't you forgotten something?" Sylvie tugged at her T-shirt.

Hélène glanced down. Her nipples were hard and pushing

through the white cotton. She shook her head. "I'm keeping this on. Just to be safe."

Sylvie frowned. "It'll only weigh you down."

"Actually, we've got a history of skin cancer in the fam—" But before she could finish her sentence, Sylvie grabbed her hand and broke into a run.

"Whatever. *On y va!*" she yelled, pulling Hélène.

"Aaaiiie!" shouted Hélène, feeling the tender soles of her feet scorching over the hot sand.

Once they reached the water, Sylvie dropped Hélène's hand and dove into the ocean. She resurfaced like a dolphin.

Hélène pouted as she tiptoed into the cold water with her arms suspended in the air. "It's freezing!"

"*Pas du tout.* Your toes are just sensitive. Dive in, you'll see. It's incredible!" gushed Sylvie as she sliced head-first into the waves.

Hélène clenched her teeth and advanced one centimeter at a time. *Mince. This is really not my idea of fun. I'm turning into an icicle.* As soon as the water reached her thighs, she stopped. Shivering, she observed Sylvie swimming circles around her.

When Sylvie's body brushed against her leg, Hélène wondered what part of her body it was. It was so soft. *Most likely a breast.* She shivered even more. Then it happened again. Hélène felt strong vibrations run through her body. *Underwater vibes*, she mused as her eyes caught flashes of white under a dark, muscular back. Through the ripples, the body looked like a shark.

Hélène bit her lip. When Sylvie finally came up for air, Hélène blurted, "Let me remind you, I'm not a big fat Greek grouper like you."

"Who are you calling a Greek grouper? You're going to pay for this, *kopela!*" Diving into the water, Sylvie skimmed the ocean floor with a frog-like thrust, resurfacing before Hélène. "This is what big wild ocean fish do to baby city guppies." She splashed Hélène's face with seawater.

Hélène covered her eyes. Her T-shirt, now wet, fully revealed the curves of her breasts. Her erect nipples were pointing directly at Sylvie. Drops of seawater streamed off their tips.

"*Arrête*, Sylvie. You're drowning me!"

"That's the idea!" teased Sylvie, still splashing.

Before Sylvie could catch her, Hélène collapsed. "Why are you so mean?" She gasped as her sobbing face entered the water.

Sylvie gently lifted Hélène and held onto her tightly. "I was just playing. I didn't realize...*Mince*. How could I be so stupid? *Je suis désolée*, my city guppy. I'd never want to hurt you. I adore you."

Just then, the sun's rays highlighted their glistening, entwined bodies in the ocean. Sylvie cupped Hélène's face in her hands, peered into her moist eyes, and kissed her tenderly on the lips.

"I adore you too," Hélène replied, taking a deep breath and kissing Sylvie back. Their tongues mingled; awkwardness turned to tenderness, which turned to passion. Sylvie attacked Hélène's throat with her lips while the two women grabbed at each other with their hungry hands, pulling their vibrating bodies together as the pair descended underwater.

About the Author

Ever since Mickey Brent was little, she knew she would write books. She has always had an insatiable curiosity about human psychology and what makes people tick. She began penning adventure stories as soon as she could hold a pencil. She would pretend she was a famous author by creating colorful little picture books and selling them to her brothers and neighborhood kids for a dime apiece.

As an adult, Mickey worked as a freelance artist and writer for various editorial publications in San Francisco. When the travel bug bit her, she relocated to several countries in Europe, where she became a translator and language teacher and studied creative writing. Mickey has finally settled down, to the astonishment of family and friends, after thriving for two decades as a globetrotter. Through the adventures of her fictional characters, Mickey's aim is to provide readers with delicious entertainment as well as glimpses of her favorite cities and cultures around the world. She relies on her linguistic and teaching skills to fund her writing passion and spends her free time learning exotic languages, drawing, taking photos, and jotting down crazy anecdotes from her travel experiences in faraway lands.

For more information about Mickey, visit www.mickeybrent.com.

Books Available From Bold Strokes Books

Change in Time by Robyn Nyx. Working in the past is hell on your future. The Extractor series: Book Two. (978-162639-880-1)

Love After Hours by Radclyffe. When Gina Antonelli agrees to renovate Carrie Longmire's new house, she doesn't welcome Carrie's overtures at friendship or her own unexpected attraction. A Rivers Community Novel. (978-163555-090-0)

Nantucket Rose by CF Frizzell. Maggie Jordan can't wait to convert a historic Nantucket home into a B&B, but doesn't expect to fall for mariner Ellis Chilton, who has more claim to the house than Maggie realizes. (978-163555-056-6)

Picture Perfect by Lisa Moreau. Falling in love wasn't supposed to be part of the stakes for Olive and Gabby, rival photographers in the competition of a lifetime. (978-162639-975-4)

Set the Stage by Karis Walsh. Actress Emilie Danvers takes the stage again in Ashland, Oregon, little realizing that landscaper Arden Philips is about to offer her a very personal romantic lead role. (978-163555-087-0)

Strike a Match by Fiona Riley. When their attempts at matchmaking fizzle out, firefighter Sasha and reluctant millionairess Abby find themselves turning to each other to strike a perfect match. (978-162639-999-0)

The Price of Cash by Ashley Bartlett. Cash Braddock is doing her best to keep her business afloat, stay out of jail, and avoid Detective Kallen. It's not working. (978-162639-708-8)

Under Her Wing by Ronica Black. At Angel's Wings Rescue, dogs are usually the ones saved, but when quiet Kassandra Haden meets outspoken owner Jayden Beaumont, the two stubborn women just might end up saving each other. (978-163555-077-1)

Underwater Vibes by Mickey Brent. When Hélène, a translator in Brussels, Belgium, meets Sylvie, a young Greek photographer and swim coach, unsettling feelings hijack Hélène's mind and body—even her poems. (978-163555-002-3)

A Date to Die by Anne Laughlin. Someone is killing people close to Detective Kay Adler, who must look to her own troubled past for a suspect. There she finds more than one person seeking revenge against her. (978-163555-023-8)

Captured Soul by Laydin Michaels. Can Kadence Munroe save the woman she loves from a twisted killer, or will she lose her to a collector of souls? (978-162639-915-0)

Dawn's New Day by TJ Thomas. Can Dawn Oliver and Cam Cooper, two women who have loved and lost, open their hearts to love again? (978-163555-072-6)

Definite Possibility by Maggie Cummings. Sam Miller is just out for good times, but Lucy Weston makes her realize happily ever after is a definite possibility. (978-162639-909-9)

Eyes Like Those by Melissa Brayden. Isabel Chase and Taylor Andrews struggle between love and ambition from the writers' room on one of Hollywood's hottest TV shows. (978-163555-012-2)

Heart's Orders by Jaycie Morrison. Helen Tucker and Tee Owens escape hardscrabble lives to careers in the Women's Army Corps, but more than their hearts are at risk as friendship blossoms into love. (978-163555-073-3)

Hiding Out by Kay Bigelow. Treat Dandridge is unaware that her life is in danger from the murderer who is hunting the woman she's falling in love with, Mickey Heiden. (978-162639-983-9)

Omnipotence Enough by Sophia Kell Hagin. Can the tiny tool that abducted war veteran Jamie Gwynmorgan accidentally acquires help her escape an unknown enemy to reclaim her stolen life and the woman she deeply loves? (978-163555-037-5)

Lessons in Desire by MJ Williamz. Can a summer love stand a four-month hiatus and still burn hot? (978-163555-019-1)